FOUR PLUS FIVE

To David H.
with wishes for health
and happiness

[signature]

Aug 8, 2010

FOUR PLUS FIVE

by

Mark Strauss

Copyright © 2009
Marek Mann Publishing
332 Zepp Road
Maurertown, Virginia 22644
(540) 459-4215
mstrauss@shentel.net

Library of Congress Control Number: 2009922073
ISBN: 978-0-9789958-1-2

Printed by
WINCHESTER PRINTERS, INC.
Winchester, Virginia

Printed on acid-free paper

I thank Augie, Donna, and Laura for their support and inspiration as I struggled with the manuscript. Ultimately, I thank my editor Ligaya Figueras, who assisted me with the creation of this book.

I dedicate this book to the memory of the Jewish residents of Lwow who were brutally murdered during the German occupation and to those who were beaten to death in Poland after the liberation. More importantly, in writing this book I remember and honor my Polish and Ukrainian neighbors who often risked their lives to help us.
May the murdered Jews and the
righteous gentiles rest in peace.

Prologue

"Watch that machine, Edziu. Don't get hurt."

My grandmother cautioned me as I inserted a long triangular scrap of thick sheet metal between the monstrous jaws of a sheet metal bender. I pulled down on the huge handle bar and the upper jaw overlapped the lower jaw just enough to bend my scrap neatly in the middle, giving it a right angle configuration.

"What are you making?"

"A sword, Grandma."

"Be very careful. That tip is very sharp. You might get hurt."

"Yes, Grandma."

"Did you do your homework, Edziu?"

"Not yet, Grandma. I am supposed to know how to add and subtract all the way to ten and I know all that—it's easy. Four plus five is nine. Right, Grandma?"

"Yes, so what's the problem?"

"The teacher told us that tomorrow we have to tell her what we get by adding four men to five women. What do you get when you mix men with women? Sometimes she is like that—a bit odd. What do you think the answer is, Grandma?"

"Well, nine…" Grandma flushed with embarrassment.

"Pani Edelman, Pani Edelman," called an apprentice from the front of the shop. "A customer just walked in. She wants to order a two-liter milk can. Can you come now and give her the price?"

My grandmother walked to the front of the shop, leaving me with all those wonderful metal scraps. Another worker was busy tending the fire that burned in a niche in the wall. An acrid smell of soldering flux pervaded the large room despite the back door having been propped wide open to the courtyard. The worker was using a bellow to blow air at the charcoal and keep it red hot. Two soldering irons among the ambers were already glowing yellowish orange. They were almost ready.

There were so many interesting activities and tools in my grandfather's sheet metal shop. My grandfather was a master in a sheet metal guild which entitled him to have his own shop and to contract for any jobs within the purview of the guild. He also had the right to employ and train apprentices and journeymen.

The sheet metal guild was large and prosperous. In the second largest town in Poland, where all the roofs were made of sheet metal, there were always plenty of repairs and a goodly number of new construction jobs. In winter, after a heavy snowfall, Grandpa's workers were kept busy shoveling snow off the roofs.

Members of the guild were mostly Jewish. The Jewish domination of metal mongering in town dated back to Middle Ages when Jews were known to manufacture weapons for defense of the town and for commerce.

The roofs of the town were my grandfather's domain— he himself didn't labor anymore. Rather, he supervised several apprentices and three journeymen, one of whom was my father.

My grandmother's kingdom was the shop. She ruled over two apprentices who were mending myriads of enameled pots, pans, skillets and other iron utensils. To get me interested in the family business, my father and my grandfather would occasionally ask me to climb up on a roof with them to watch how the tinned metal sheets or rolls were joined together and attached to the rafters. However, this wasn't my thing. I had a fear of heights; a sloping roof was an anathema to me.

It was the shop with its several machines for fashioning and slicing metal sheets that attracted me. I also liked to observe how skillfully the helpers pounded the copper rivets into the holes of pots and then finished them by melting tin with soldering irons. In the shop I was amused and safe.

"Edek, another seven years and you will be fourteen. Then Pani Edelman will put you to work, no? You will be like your father, no, Edek? Now, aren't you going to flatten that jagged hunk you created so that it looks like a real sword? Wait a minute and I will reset the press for you." The apprentice spoke to me in Yiddish as he straightened himself out and wiped the sweat from his forehead.

"Thank you, Samuel." I switched into Polish, which was really my language. I understood Yiddish but could speak only a few phrases. Most of the older Jews in town could communicate in both languages. The younger generation, like my parents, spoke entirely in Polish, even to each other.

"All I have to do now is to sand off the excess of tin and the pot will be ready, even for cooking sauerkraut. Surely, your grandma will not find fault with my repair."

"Yes. Grandma is very keen on good work. We have our name to protect—I heard my grandfather say so."

"One more pot done, but look at all the ones that are lying around waiting. We do have a good business, no?" Samuel answered again in Yiddish. He picked up an enamel wash basin and examined its rusty bottom. He began to whistle a joyful tune as I whirled my sword around me and thought happily of how envious my friends would be when I brought my new weapon to our courtyard.

"I was thinking about your devious teacher," Samuel's words interrupted my daydream. "You can't add things that are not the same, no? Pots go with pots, pans with pans. She is trying to trick you children."

"But men and women are *people*. Together they are nine *people*. Right, Samuel? We Jews are people. The Poles and Ukrainians—our neighbors—they are all people too. Aren't they, Samuel?"

Samuel nodded without looking up as he focused on repairing the basin. He began to whistle again. I lifted my sword and began to slash the air with it while my thoughts turned to my people, my family.

My grandparents, and consequently my parents, were middle class. Not rich—but they lived fairly well. The shop was at the center of our lives. It was a block away from a large farmers' market. We saw a constant flow of peasant women who brought their wares for repair. We also made milk cans and other containers to their specifications.

"Samuel, have you finished that pot? Edek, don't disturb him." My grandmother's voice boomed as she returned from the front and addressed us both.

"No, Pani Edelman. Edek doesn't disturb me. I am trying to teach him some tricks of our trade."

After glancing approvingly at the newly mended pot, Grandma turned to me.

"Have you eaten your lunch, Edziu? Probably not, huh?"

"No, Grandma. My mother is visiting Cousin Paula and hasn't come back yet."

"Just what I thought. Come with me to the kitchen and I will make a sandwich for you, poor child. One of the peasants just paid me in part with a cooked ham. Of course, I haven't tasted it…"

Grandma looked down at the bundle she held in her hands. The ham was wrapped in a brown paper bag and dark grease spots shone through.

"It smells delicious. God forbid that your grandfather Zalel should see me feed you ham."

"Yes, ham sounds good, Grandma. Do you still have that horseradish that we had for Passover?" Horseradish, mustard, and pickles of all sorts were delicacies for me, and Grandma knew it.

The sandwich turned out to be a plate with slices of dark bread, hunks of ham, mustard, and pickled mushrooms. All of it was slopped together but it tasted great.

"When is Grandpa coming back?" I asked.

Grandma ignored my question and began a critical dissertation on my mother for whom, I am sure, she had affection but seldom exhibited it. In her heart, she did care for my pretty but grievously handicapped mother. After all, it was my mother who gave birth to her only grandson.

"Your mother doesn't feed you enough. She is too busy with her social life. Your mother and her cousin Paula are fine ones. They are our Yiddish aristocracy," she began sarcastically and laughed, showing gaping holes between her teeth.

Grandma still had a few of her own teeth remaining at critical locations, which allowed her to bite and chew, albeit carefully. No golden teeth for her, she used to brag. Well, she wasn't quite truthful because, on occasion, I could see a glitter of gold in the back of her mouth.

What exasperated Grandma was that my mother was not an exemplary housekeeper and this, she reasoned, was because Mother's family was bourgeois. My mother's brother was a respected physician and a major in the Polish Army with connections leading all the way up to Marshall Pilsudski, a Polish autocrat. Cousin Paula's husband was a prominent dermatologist with a burgeoning practice.

Cousin Paula lived a block down the street and Mother visited her almost daily. It seems that many things of importance to me were a block away: my elementary school, my piano teacher, Uncle Zygmunt's large apartment where he also stored some of his plumbing equipment. I was welcome to browse among his assorted valves and pipes. Uncle Zygmunt, my father's brother, was a plumbing contractor. He had earned his diploma from a prestigious German technical school; consequently, his apartment had the most modern bathroom and toilet in town.

In fact, his toilet was for me like a hydrant is for a dog: it was my pit stop. The gloss of the white tiles and metallic luster of the fixtures were most inviting to me and I relieved myself there frequently. One piece of equipment fascinated me. My uncle called it a "bidet," which, I think, is a French word. It was shaped similar to a toilet bowl with a spout from which water sprinkled vertically upward like a fountain. It puzzled me and excited my imagination: What and who was it designed to wash?

"That's enough! Don't play with it, Edziu! See, you made the floor wet. Go outside and play there. Not here."

That was that. Aunt Sarah gently castigated me and forced me to leave, but only until next time, when again I experimented with the bidet, being more cautious in regulating the surge of water.

My family life did extend beyond a one-block radius. Father's Uncle Zuckerberg had a unique textile shop in the commercial center of the town. His store was located in a vast enclosed mall that served as a passage between two main streets. I guess there was some truth to what Grandma said about my mother. Our visits to Uncle Zuckerberg's store had definite social overtones. Mother and Manka Zuckerberg, my father's spinster cousin, would talk for hours about this one and that one, about the card games they played and what kind of future the gypsy woman predicted for them.

I spent my time observing the habits of clergymen of various religions who came to the store to buy ecclesiastical textiles. They spent hours examining the heavy, brocaded silver- and gold-threaded materials that were stacked from floor to ceiling like horizontal books on shelves. It was a visual feast, but even feasts get boring to a seven-year-old boy.

"Mama, let's go. I want to go home."

"Just wait. Don't you have anything to do? You know, Manka, that man—the lawyer from Warsaw—he could be a good catch. The gypsy did say that the King of Spades is favorably disposed to you and that a journey awaits you. Cards never lie. He is dark-complexioned, isn't he?"

"Mama, I want to go home. I have to practice my handwriting. My teacher assigned us calligraphy for homework," I fibbed. I just wanted to get home and play with the other boys.

"Wait, Edziu. Five more minutes. Go buy yourself a comic book." She reached down into her handbag which lay next to her feet and pulled out her coin purse. "Here is ten groszy," she said, handing me the small coin as she continued her conversation with Manka, "I have a feeling that before long there will be a wedding in your future, Manka."

I looked down at the money in my hand. Why not try? I thought.

"But, Mama, Grandma gives me always fifteen groszy," I urged.

"Grandma is certainly spoiling you. Here, take twenty."

Prince Valiant, Katzenmeyer Twins, and *Superman* were my favorites. I spent many a ten-groszy on those comic books, enraptured by the twists and turns in their adventures. I also was able to fill my piggy bank with many five-groszy coins saved from Grandma's overpayments.

My piggy bank profited far more from family card games. Sechs und Sechtig, a card game that translates to "Sixty-six," was our family disease. It infected every family member on my father's side except my grandparents. My mother's relatives, decidedly fewer in number but of greater import, were immune to that contagion. As Grandma castigated them: they were blue bloods and nothing as vulgar as gambling would suit them.

Sundays were dedicated to "Sixty-six." During the winter, between twenty and thirty relatives would squeeze into Uncle Zuckerberg's apartment. Some waited for their turn at the table; some were there to "kibitz" or simply to eat delicacies prepared by Zuckerberg's wife and socialize. In summer, the action was transferred to a spacious outdoor restaurant in a park on a hill that overlooked town. When the weather was nice, our group would generally swell with more family and friends.

There, among the many tables and benches, a picnic atmosphere prevailed. Children played, adults sunned themselves, some played ball games, and of course everyone ate and drank. The big wooden table where they played cards was the centerpiece, with Uncle Zuckerberg presiding and my mother occupying her traditional position on his left. My place was on my father's lap opposite Uncle Zuckerberg. My job was to collect and dispense coins for my father. I was paid for "helping" him: For every ante he won, my share was ten groszy. I did not share in his losses, though, and my piggy bank was assured of getting fuller and fuller.

Cards and coins slid across the table while shrieking voices—sometimes even harsh remarks—bounced from player to player.

"Sixty-six!" yelled my mother pointing to cards on the table. Her face was flush with excitement. She loved to gamble.

I, too, was in my element. I was in the middle of my family, feeling happy, sound and secure. "Sixty-six" in the summer was even better than family Passover dinners. When all of us gathered in the park, there was little seriousness and mostly a joy of living—yet there was fear.

"Look, Zuckerberg."

Uncle Zygmunt pointed in the direction of several young men who wore the insignia of a fascistic fraternity on their academic caps and brandished canes. They were not picnicking. They stood together and surveyed people at the tables, looking for trouble.

"There may be a problem."

"I hope they don't disturb us. I have several short pipes under the table," Uncle Zygmunt addressed my father and pointed below. "Just in case," he added.

"Just keep playing. Don't pay attention to them," responded my father. "Shove me one of those pipes and give the other ones to Heniek and Zuckerberg," I sensed the tightening of his arm muscles as he loosened his hold on me.

"Get down, Edek. If anything happens, crawl under the table."

"Sixty-six!" My mother screamed ecstatically and got up from the chair. She beckoned to a waiter and then calmly asked around the table, "Who wants kefir? Who wants seltzer? I'm paying."

"I want kefir, Mama." The sour goat's milk, something like yogurt, was my treat. Soda, with or without syrup, I could leave for the adults to enjoy.

"Here! They are coming!" hissed Uncle Zuckerberg, laying down his cards.

My father, Zuckerberg, Zygmunt, Cousin Heniek, and even the spinster Manka slowly reached down and grasped for the pipes. All the while, they talked in a casual tone. A passerby would think nothing was amiss. How I would have liked to have had in my hands the sword I had fashioned a few weeks earlier!

The group of fascistic Polish students, EN-DEKS, passed within a few feet of the table. They murmured something about Jews, but that was all. They must have sensed our spirit of defiance or saw the strong, muscular arms of my relatives. Perhaps they saw Jews at other tables and decided that the odds were against them.

During those moments, I loved my family, my people. I was proud of being one of them. And the cold kefir tasted better than usual.

Chapter I. Germany Strikes

It was 1941 when Germany struck Poland. I was thirteen, practically fourteen. Donia was fifteen. I was Jewish. Donia was a Polish Catholic.

The ensuing three-year German occupation and its aftermath brought torment and murder to us—to me, to Donia, and to the rest of the Jews and even some of the non-Jews who lived with us in our apartment house in the medieval city of Lwow. That period was indescribably sordid and cruel for us, yet love was also our portion.

Today I am old and decrepit, living in America and awaiting death, the ultimate savior. Donia is just a beautiful memory that makes my last days bearable.

+ + + + + + + + +

The onslaught began very early one Sunday morning in June of 1941 when the German army lashed its might at the unsuspecting Soviets. At that stage of World War II, Lwow was under the domination of the Soviet Union. More clearly, after Poland was obliterated by the German Army in September of 1939, Lwow, a Polish town—my town—was incorporated into the Ukrainian Socialistic Republic.

That Sunday morning, as every morning under the Soviet domination, I was sleeping in the same room with my parents. The Soviet government had requisitioned two rooms of our four-room apartment for Soviet Army personnel. We had to squeeze into the two small remaining rooms.

That morning, all hell broke loose as the Luftwaffe appeared over the town, bombing and machine-gunning. The Red Army and the Red Air Force were almost completely caught off guard. Though feeble, their antiaircraft fire from the ground caused an incredible ruckus. Shrapnel broke windows. Craggy bits of falling shrapnel peppered the sheet metal roof of our apartment house and added to the din of exploding bombs and the drone of airplane engines. I was excited because the airplanes were flying low over the buildings; one very large one had red stars on its wings; the small one chasing it had black crosses.

"Come on Red Star, escape!" I yelled, as my father motioned me to get away from the window.

Today, reclining on a sofa in a small room of a nursing home, I test my memory of those long gone years. With eyes shut, I try to recall important events, but also many trivial images. When I open my eyes and look out the window, some unbelievable images shimmer and vibrate with many vivid hues, enlivened by the rays of the sun as it sets beyond the Blue Ridge Mountains. Are they my fantasies? Am I hallucinating? At my age, nightmares and reality diffuse into each other, resulting in a colorful kaleidoscope of crystals; their shapes form, dissolve and reform. Some crystalline facets are black. Then my vision blurs. No matter. When I am able to focus again, I write down the memories and describe those fantastic images. The doctors tell me that, in addition to more serious problems, I also suffer from an optical migraine. I wonder if any other of the elderly residents here suffers from the same problem. Be that as it may, I know that at least my memory is fairly good, although some episodes simply evade me.

Perhaps I don't want to remember some of them. Like, I don't remember how I looked at thirteen or fourteen, and certainly not what I wore to bed, as that memorable Sunday dawned. I was a typical boy; I paid no attention to what I wore, and I certainly didn't want to know what my mother wore at night. I would have been terribly embarrassed if I had seen her even partially undressed, so I always looked away before we went to bed and again in the morning when we dressed. What my mother looked like then, I don't remember. I only remember her face from the two photos that I still carry in my wallet.

The pictures were taken prior to the war. She had a lovely face, light brown hair, and blue eyes. My mother was crippled. She was born without a left hand because the umbilical cord had tied itself around her left wrist. Of course, at that time I didn't know all that. I only saw the five tiny, rounded stumps where her wrist was supposed to be. No wonder that I looked at her as little as possible. On that fateful Sunday, however, I saw—and still see—my mother clearly: in that single instance, fearfully clutching my father's thigh with her right hand as he hurriedly got up from their bed.

"Kurt, what is happening? Are the Soviets having one of their war exercises again?" she asked.

My father did not answer. Dashing to the window, he shouted at me, "Edek, get under the bed. Quickly! Under our bed!"

In contrast to how spotty is my vision of my mother, I remember my father well. I see him on that morning in his *kalesony*, long johns with strings to tie the leggings around the ankles. Men wore them throughout the year. In winter, they wore ones made of heavy material; in summertime, they donned lightweight *kalesony*. My father's chest was bare as he came to the window to yank me away and push me under the bed. He was a muscular man with the arms and chest of a laborer—and a soldier. He was a teenager when he fought as an infantryman in the war against the Bolsheviks during the formation of the Polish state. Later, he was promoted to lieutenancy in the Polish Army Reserve. When Germany struck Poland, he was working for my grandfather as a sheet metal journeyman.

As the nearby burst of a shell rattled our windows, the door to our bedroom was shoved open. My head was protruding from under the bed and the door slammed into it hard. Grisha, a Soviet airman who occupied one of the requisitioned rooms, stepped over me as I was holding my head in my hands. He screamed at my father and gestured toward the window.

"These are not maneuvers! This is war! Those bastards sneakily, brutally, are attacking us!"

Grisha ran back to the antechamber, draped himself with his overcoat, and raced half-dressed to the staircase, still yelling. "We will teach them a lesson. *Skatina*, cattle, bugger fascists!"

Irina, the military nurse who occupied the other bedroom, ran into our room. She bent down toward me and kissed me on the head.

"Remember me. We will be back. We should not have trusted Germans."

Irina was very nice to me. She was always showing me the letters she received from her nephew in Odessa. He drew excellent sketches of the ships that he saw entering Odessa's harbor. I guess that I was a surrogate nephew to Irina. With tears in her eyes, she ran downstairs. I never saw Irina or Grisha again.

We spent that night with most of our neighbors in the cellar which was supposed to have sheltered us from bombs. Perhaps it would have saved our lives in case of an indirect hit. Fortunately, it never came to the test. Throughout the night, we heard the frequent drone of aircraft and antiaircraft shell explosions. The Germans were focusing their attention on targets farther east, deeper in the Soviet Union. The adults tried to maintain composure and even tried to sleep on the mattresses they brought with them.

There was no sleeping for us children. We had immense fun running in and out between the dank, dimly lit cellar and the dark staircase. We were bumping into each other, jostling and pretending to be ghouls from the underworld. Those of us who disobeyed our parents and ventured into the courtyard were treated to an outdoor display of crisscrossing search lights that stabbed the night sky in search of German planes. The beams of light vigorously scanned the sky until midnight. With every succeeding hour, the number of beams lessened: the Soviets were abandoning their posts.

They weren't the only ones. Uncle Zygmunt was abandoning his wife Sarah. The following morning, she ran crying toward my father with her hands flaying wildly around her. She grabbed him by the arm, shook him, and pointed toward the balcony of her apartment.

"There! He is leaving me! Your brother is leaving me. Tell him…I am his wife. I need…"

"Get hold of yourself, Sarah. Where is Zygmunt?"

"He's cramming his backpack with his stuff. He's leaving me."

"You mean he wants to run away with the Soviets? East?"

"How can he do it? He is selfish! What am I to do, Kurt?"

"Go with him."

"I have my parents. I must take care of them. I can't leave them, you know that. Besides, I am sure that the Germans will not be as bad as some would like us to believe. They cannot be as brutal as the Soviets were."

Sarah stilled herself and wiped the tears from her eyes. She dropped her hands in dejection and lowered her head.

"He has no…qualms…about leaving," she stammered pitifully between sniffles. "He knows that you will…care…of Grandma and Grandpa Edelman…and—"

"Yes," my father interrupted her. "I have seriously considered running too, but I have my own family."

"Well, Zygmunt may think that he's being brave, but you are braver by staying here and taking care of everyone who depends on you."

"I have no choice really. Grandma and Grandpa and the rest of you need me. I must stay, come what may."

And so, Uncle Zygmunt, wearing a pack on his back and holding a small suitcase in his hand, merged with a stream of bedraggled Soviet infantrymen and vehicles as they retreated eastward.

They departed to the tune of small arms fire as they tried to defend themselves from nationalistic Ukrainian snipers.

Although he survived the war, I did not see Uncle Zygmunt again. And three sordid, cruel years would pass before I would again see armed soldiers of the Red Army.

Chapter II. Occupation Begins

⌒

But I did see plenty of Germans. That day—maybe it was the next, I can't remember for sure—the German Army rolled into town along with their Hungarian allies. The soldiers looked hardy, well dressed, and cheerful. Their weapons were powerful. In addition to tanks, half-tracked vehicles, and numerous trucks, came battalions of motorcyclists and bicyclists. It was a seemingly endless procession of military might. In the wake of this highly mobile army came a second echelon of Germans. Captain Erich Stumme took possession of the two rooms in our apartment that were vacated by the Soviets. With him came his wife, Yanka, and son, Yacek. Yanka was Pan Burek's niece. Pan Burek lived with Pani Cwik—they weren't married as far as I know—but they were our neighbors, they shared an apartment across the hall from us. Stumme's son was the same age as me. But who was Captain Stumme?

Who were some of the other residents in our apartment house? Who were the Jews and gentiles? Men and women, boys and girls. They were the people of my childhood—all mixed together. We lived under the same roof, our fates interwoven for good and for ill.

Our apartment house was unique because, among its residents, four Jewish males were intimately involved with at least five gentile females. If you believe in one-to-one ratio, it didn't add up. Moreover, that arrangement didn't make sense because it was an era of rampant anti-Semitism; the Nazi slogan of *rassen shande* was fashionable and permeated Europe. "The races must not mix! Jews must not pollute the Aryans with their blood!" spouted the Nazis.

It was a time when nothing really added up. Who were those four men and five women who did not conform to the fascistic view of the world? Were they duped? Were they simple-minded romantics? Were they sex crazed or were they idealists, truly in love?

Four of the nine were murdered by the brutal Germans and Ukrainians. One was killed by a few vicious Poles. Two died a natural death. One, my father—who lived a long time—was so traumatized by the events of that brutal era that he never talked about the past. My father wrote assiduously while we were hidden later on during the occupation. He brought his journals to America. I read them before he destroyed them during a fit of depression.

So there is no one else left but me in my sorry despondency to relate the tale of those nine sexually aberrant individuals in our apartment house. Well, actually Donia Laskawa and I will tell you the story because we were among the nine. It is from my reminiscences and from what I gleamed from my father's journals and from Donia's personal papers, on which she faithfully, albeit hastily, scribbled, that our story evolves.

Chapter III. Captain Stumme Enters Our Lives

Whenever I think of those early days of the German occupation, Captain Erich Stumme forces himself into my memory. In August of 1941, when he and his orderly entered our apartment to claim the two requisitioned rooms, we were awed by the crisp, well-fitting uniform of an officer of the Organization Todt, the German Army's Corps of Engineers. He was of medium height and stocky build, with the brush-like mustachios and brusque manner of a conqueror. He made no small talk but told my father that his family would be arriving in Lwow within a few days and that we had better see to it that his rooms were cleaned and furnished properly.

"Burn or throw away all that stinking Russian junk they left behind. Make sure that you leave the windows open to get rid of their odor," he told us sternly, pointing to the door of Irina's former room.

Irina, who was nearly of retirement age, used cosmetics galore to make herself more attractive, and the sweet smell pervaded her room as well as the antechamber where we all stood.

Captain Stumme gestured toward the doors to two cubicles: the toilet and the bathroom.

"Make sure that these are super-clean," he told us. "You will use the bathtub only if my wife gives you permission."

Fortunately, he said nothing about our rights to use the toilet. Did he forget to do so? But then, what would we have done if…? He had to put up with us but maybe he thought that it would not be for long.

We should have been scared of *Kapitein* Stumme, especially by his armband with the swastika that identified the members of Organization Todt, but we weren't. Perhaps because he spoke Polish, but mainly because Pan Burek told us ahead of time that Captain Stumme was his in-law. Pan Burek intimated to my father that he was not fond of Captain Stumme because Stumme, being an admirer of Hitler, chose to proclaim his German ancestry and became a *Volksdeutche*. That is, he officially became an ethnic German and a Nazi to boot. To me, at first, all that Captain Stumme needed to do in order to be a photo model of a Nazi was to raise his hand in Nazi salute and utter "Heil Hitler." I never saw him do it. For that matter, in all the months that followed we saw very little of him. But every day, we interacted with Pani Yanka, his wife, and Yacek, his son. And we all did use the common toilet facilities more or less amicably.

From that day when Captain Stumme first entered our antechamber—as well as our lives—our apartment became "the Stummes' apartment."

On that day, I remember as Captain Stumme turned completely around on his heels, his eyes sweeping all six doors that lead from the antechamber.

"Yes, it will be adequate," he said in Polish to no one in particular. Then, turning to the orderly, he said in German, "The directive. You will nail it to the door, of course."

"*Yawohl, mein Kapitein.*"

The orderly, who so far stood motionless, stirred, bowed to Stumme, and took a rolled document out of the briefcase.

"I will need a hammer and some small nails, *mein Kapitein*." He bowed again to Stumme and then turned to my father: "You, Jew! Get me a hammer and nails. Damn you, Jew. Get!"

This jolted my father, who immediately entered our room to obey the command as Captain Stumme sat down on the low stool that we used to put on our boots. He relaxed, took out a cigar, and chewed it. He lit the cigar and threw the match at a spittoon but missed. The orderly bent down, picked it up, and threw it down the rather narrow hole of the jar.

After a while, Stumme raised his head and resurveyed the antechamber. His eyes came to rest on my mother as she stood by me. She held my hand in her good hand, her maimed hand was hidden behind her.

"What are you hiding in your hand?" he asked sternly and pointed to my mother with the cigar.

"Nothing, nothing. It's just that I have no hand," my mother blurted out with tears in her eyes. She held out her arm, exposing the grotesque stubs on her wrist.

It was a traumatic moment for me, almost as if my mother was forced to undress right then and there. But it also had an unsuspected effect on Stumme. He murmured something, lowered his eyes, turned his head away from us, and threw away the practically untouched cigar.

My father returned with the hammer and nails and handed them to the orderly. Stumme, still sitting, turned to my father and said, "Thank you, Panie Edelman." The softness in his voice surprised me.

So it wasn't "You, Jew" but "Mister Edelman," I thought to myself.

I looked at the sitting Stumme with his head down, cradled in his palms. At that moment, even the uniform appeared to me to be somewhat crumpled. He seemed to be a different man. In spite of the swastika and the black riding boots, he appeared quite human, like an apprehensive actor waiting for his cue to enter the stage; an actor aptly dressed to perform in a bloody World War II drama; a genteel man, in fact—just ill-suited to his role.

Chapter IV. View from the Third Floor

"Don't go out on the street. Don't go downstairs, Donia! There is a German truck—some sort of military vehicle—out there. It just stopped in front of our gate. Look, Donia!" Pani Laskawa pressed her head lightly against the front window. The glass was cracked, having been hit by flying shrapnel. It was held together by tape that was peeling at the edges and getting dirtier by the day.

"There are three Germans with swastika armbands. One of them in the back seat must be an officer. He is getting out. The car has a pendant with a swastika and something written—"

"It says something in German. 'Org—' something, and then 'Todt.' Oh, Mama! That means 'death' in German!" Donia chimed in nervously.

"They are probably looking for Jews, but don't you go out! You are just fifteen but you look older and you have a nice figure. Who knows what they would do. Let's get away from the window. I don't want them to see us."

Donia and her mother retreated back into their vestibule. They placed their ears against the door to the staircase and listened anxiously. "They are coming up. I think there are only two of them."

Indeed, heavy boot steps were just passing the first floor where Tusiek Shapiro and Pani Ala lived and practiced dentistry. Tusiek was a dental technician and a Jew. Pani Ala was a Polish dentist.

"They are coming to the second floor. Are they going to take the Edelmans and Edek? I can hear them knocking. They are knocking on the door, they aren't kicking it in," Pani Laskawa commented. "Maybe—"

The fact that they were not banging on the door and yelling at the Edelmans was a good sign, thought Donia.

"So perhaps they will not take the Edelmans," she said hopefully to her mother who was still listening intently with her ear glued to the door. Donia respected the Edelman family and she was especially fond of Edek, their thirteen-year-old son.

"I can hear Pan Burek's voice. They must have entered the Edelman's apartment because I hear nothing," Pani Laskawa whispered quietly. The Laskawy family lived on the third floor, directly above the Edelmans.

Pan Laskawy, Donia's father, was a Polish prisoner of war being held somewhere in the Soviet Union. Donia's nineteen-year-old brother, Roman, spent hours maintaining his place in line at the local *bakalia* waiting for the eventual delivery of bread. Sometimes the bread arrived at the grocery store; often it didn't. Roman reported that the Edelmans and all the other Jews were often kicked out of the line, unable to buy the scarce bread. Just today they were beaten by local ruffians, he said. Sometimes Donia wondered what the Edelmans ate. There were the peasants from nearby villages who sold their produce to Jews willing to venture out into the local market, but they sold it at an exorbitant price.

"They left the apartment," Pani Laskawa announced from her listening post, breathing a sigh. "But, wait! I can hear staccato bangs. It sounds like they are nailing something."

Donia, too, heard distinct hammer blows and then the sound of boots descending the stairs. They ran quickly to the front room window and peered through the broken glass. They reached the window just in time to see two Germans walk past the gate and enter the vehicle. The driver saluted and opened the door. This time, the officer sat next to the driver and the other one, presumably his orderly, behind them. A puff of smoke belched from the exhaust pipe and they zoomed away.

Donia also zoomed away, but toward the staircase.

"Mama, I am going down," she shouted back, taking two and three steps at a time. She heard her mother remonstrating, "Don't you go. You foolish girl, come back!" But she was young and ignorant to the many dangers of the adult world. What worried her mother more was how quickly her daughter was maturing. She had seen how young men stared at her daughter. Donia had been turning heads even before she began high school, before the war, when she and Donia could still stroll peacefully down the *corso* together.

Donia reached the second floor within moments and stood before the Edelman's apartment. The door was shut, which was nothing usual, but a large tablet was nailed to the door and a certificate was attached to it: DO NOT ENTER. HERE LIVES CAPTAIN E. STUMME, ORGANIZATION TODT. Underneath were two signatures and the prominent circular stamp of an eagle holding a garlanded swastika in his talons. During the next three years they would come to know that emblem well; like the eagles of the Roman Legions, it was feared throughout most of Europe.

Chapter V. Enter the Stummes

The Captain + Yanka

"Edek, keep grinding."

My mother admonished me when I slackened from turning the handle of the small mill. Before the war, we used it for coffee beans. Now I was grinding wheat kernels into coarse grain that my mother would mix with water, flatten, and then bake on the top of a tiny wood stove in the kitchen. A few teaspoons of wheat were just enough for one small pancake. The wheat was a gift from Pani Yanka.

Captain Stumme supplied his family with ample food. Every week or so, a military truck would stop in front of our house and a German soldier would deliver a package or two to Pani Yanka. It was the best food and libations that the captain and his German cohorts could liberate on the Eastern front. Yacek Stumme did not have to grind wheat. His family had flour to make pancakes. They had lard and sugar, which they occasionally shared with us or bartered with peasants in exchange for potatoes. Cigarettes, vodka, and cognac, which often arrived in care packages, were Pani Yanka's special province; these she did not share.

Yes, having the Stumme family reside with us in the same apartment had its plusses. The greatest benefit was the imposing official certificate nailed to the door of the apartment. The German eagle with the swastika guarded us. No marauding Ukrainian policemen dared to enter our apartment. The notice on the door that "Captain Stumme Lives Here" may even have prevented an unofficial raid by German police early during the occupation. Later, however, *Einsatz Gruppen*, the Death Commandos, respected nothing in ferreting out the Jews.

Yacek was exactly my age but we were so different from one another. I was blond, blue-eyed, and willowy. He had dark hair and dark eyes, and was plump and shorter than I. He was an Aryan and I was a Jew. In the nose department, we both adhered more to the Nazi anatomical prototypes. I have a long nose, though not a bulging one; Yacek had—or if he is still alive somewhere, has—as a small, upturned, pointy nose, a common inheritance among Slavs, including Poles. Jews were described as people with large, crooked noses. In those days, I wished for a much less pronounced proboscis.

"Yacek, come upstairs. Please, Yacek, I want you upstairs. Right away, Yacek! Please, Yacek!" Pani Yanka's nagging voice resounded within the walls of our L-shaped apartment house as she stood on our kitchen balcony and looked down upon the inner courtyard where the three of us boys played.

"You'd better listen to your mama, you sissy boy. She won't love you anymore, sissy baby. Did she forget to wrap you in diapers today? If you need to piss, you better run home," Kazik cruelly jeered at Yacek.

"I will tell on you to my father next time he visits us from the front. He is a German captain and has two hundred soldiers under him," retorted Yacek, who blushed and then ran toward the staircase.

"And how many women does he have under him in bed? Ha, ha! I bet you don't know, you silly ass!" Kazik shouted a parting insult to Yacek.

We were not the proverbial "Three Musketeers," although we were approximately the same age and we lived in the same apartment house. "One for all and all for one" certainly did not apply to us. Kazik was Ukrainian but he had a Polish mother. Yacek was half-German and I was Jewish. As a result, our games often ended on a bitter note.

"You just wait till my father comes home!" shouted Yacek, slamming the door to the staircase behind him.

"Yeah? When will 'The Captain' return? Maybe never." Kazik turned to me after Yacek's departure, winking as if he knew something. "My father knows a lot of German officers. He fashions shoes for their women. They all have girls—a lot of girls—for cigarettes and food."

"Your father gets cigarettes and other goodies—plenty of stuff. He is not a girl," I remarked caustically to Kazik. He nodded in agreement and smiled ruefully.

To me, Kazik was not antagonistic, although he was bitingly sarcastic at times. I do not believe that his parents were anti-Semitic either. Kazik was just Kazik; he was simply a bitter pill. However unpleasant Kazik was, he was the last of my gentile friends who still played with me downstairs in the courtyard. My other playmates avoided me because I was a Jew. Kazik played with me even though he and his family were pro-German. They flaunted the prosperous status they achieved under the Third Reich. Kazik's father was a shoemaker who knew how to ingratiate himself to the *Wehrmacht* and police officers, both German and Ukrainian. He was Ukrainian himself and, of course, that helped a lot.

Yacek seldom played in our small courtyard where I horsed around with Kazik. Kazik was younger by a year or so, but more experienced than I in many ways. He liked rowdy games, especially with girls. Girls, girls and girls were on his mind and, if I were to believe him, they liked it when he fondled them. He was especially enamored with Lesia, the eleven-year-old daughter of a Ukrainian couple who lived on the third floor opposite Donia's apartment. Lesia Fedan was a very pretty, slight girl with curly blonde hair.

Yacek, in contrast to Kazik, frequently opted for nonphysical entertainment. Both Yacek and I must have been late bloomers. We collected stamps and coins and were more or less unaware of girls, although I always turned my head to look at Donia whenever she passed by the courtyard or came out onto the balcony.

Yacek preferred being in his family's section of the apartment or playing with me in my family's two rooms, or visiting with Pan Burek and Pani Cwik. Perhaps Pani Stumme did not want him to associate with other youngsters in the apartment house. She was inseparable from Yacek. She often hugged him and even kissed him in front of me, which I would have found frightfully embarrassing if my mother had done so to me. Pani Yanka and Yacek had a very special affection for each other and it showed.

Pani Yanka always appeared to be burdened and fearful. She seldom smiled and never laughed. To her, Yacek was the object of love—a love that she could have bestowed on his father, I think. That is, if Captain Stumme would come home from the front. Strangely, letters and packages arrived regularly, but no Captain Stumme. Sometimes I saw her talking seriously to Pan Burek, her uncle. Wisps of Pan Burek's words of solace inadvertently reached my ears.

"Don't worry, Yanka. He will take care of himself. He knows. He is a mature man, after all, with lots of experience."

"But what about Yacek? How can I protect Yacek?" whispered Pani Yanka and then, seeing me, she led Pan Burek from the kitchen and onto the balcony.

How foolish to think that Yacek, Captain Stumme's son, needed protection. After all, Yacek was a sweet, obedient boy, and more importantly, he was a gentile. People like him shouldn't need protection. Protection from what?

Chapter VI. One Less Jew

"**M**ama, Mama! There are people on the sidewalk across the street. It may be a farmer selling potatoes," Donia yelled, her head still sticking out the window.

Pani Laskawa didn't look up. She was busy threading a needle. A pile of clothes in need of mending lay on the floor beside her. It seemed to Donia that every time her mother sat down for a sewing session she would remark about their money problems.

"We cannot afford a seamstress these days," she was saying. "It was different when your father—"

"We could use potatoes," continued Donia. "The peasant probably wants a fortune for them, but people are all around him. Some have uniforms. That's curious."

Before Pani Laskawa even had a chance to poke the needle into the pincushion and come to the window, Donia had bolted out of the door and down the stairs. She didn't even slow down at the Edelman's door with the German eagle so prominently perched, guarding the entrance to what they now called "Stumme's aerie." "Eagle," in Donia's vocabulary, was that official certificate on their door. Poland, too, had an eagle for its national emblem but so did other countries. Yet, the German eagle looked so ferociously vicious to her.

Donia didn't have a chance to think why did the German eagle appeared meaner than all the other eagles as she passed the first floor. It was there that she heard familiar steps arise from the main entrance to the house. It was Tadzik, the young man that she daydreamed about. Yes, Tadzik Shoenhoffer was twenty-one, tall, dark—simply a dream boat. Here they were, alone on the stairs! He smiled mischievously and approached with outstretched arms as if to embrace her. She slowly backed up the stairs one step at a time to avoid his advances. In spite of her desires to be held by Tadzik, she resisted her impulses; a romance with Tadzik was risky to say the least. He had a reputation when it came to girls—he took them and left them.

"You silly goose, I am not going to chase you. There are other girls, prettier and more willing than you. Go, go down. I won't stop you. Go across the street for entertainment. They are beating a Jew. You might enjoy it," Tadzik teased, grinning.

Donia took one more step up, backwards, when Tadzik's mother, Pani Shoenhoffer, opened the door. She was always suspicious of noises in the hallway. A disapproving look crossed her face and Tadzik brushed passed Donia and up the remaining stairs to the Shoenhoffer's apartment. Pani Shoenhoffer shut the door loudly leaving Donia to sort out her feelings in the dimly lit staircase.

How different was Tadzik from Bolek, his younger brother! Bolek was shorter, fatter, and less attractive than Tadzik. Bolek was much more kind to her though. That must have been his Polish mother's blood in him. But they were all *Volksdeutche*, ethnic Germans, their masters. Well, Tadzik certainly behaved like that. The seeds of their German father had sprouted well in Tadzik.

Before another thought could enter Donia's mind, she was on the street, then across it. She craned her neck to see what was happening in the center of the group of people.

A man stood in the middle surrounded by onlookers. At first, she could not see him because he was either kneeling or sitting on the flagstones. But when he rose from the sidewalk she could see the tall man's head above the crowd. He held it in his hands, protecting it from the blows of those next to him. Blood trickled from a gash on his forehead; more blood flowed from his nose onto his hands. Only one of his eyes was open; the other was hidden by large swellings on his face. He screamed for mercy in a shrill voice.

"I am not a communist! My father is a tailor. You must know him—there, around the corner! Please, please. I beg you, I am inno—"

A blow to his mouth from a bamboo cane jolted him. He staggered momentarily but steadied himself and remained erect.

"Matko Boska," Donia blurted out loudly. Saint Mary, Mother of God! What are they doing? Who is that unfortunate man? He looked familiar. Her brain raced as she frantically tried to remember who he was. There weren't that many tall men in the neighborhood.

"Who is he?" Donia said aloud again.

"Just a Jew. They helped the Soviets to kill us. Did you hear what they did to our prisoners at Brigidki, the downtown jail? These Jews and Commies bludgeoned our people," a woman standing next to her explained quietly into her ear.

A man wearing the uniform of a railroad worker turned toward them and with a glee exclaimed, "Good! Christ be blessed! There will be one less Jew." Donia watched as both he and the woman crossed themselves and bowed their heads in the direction of a statue of Saint Anthony holding a Jewish baby in his arms. Baby Jesus. Didn't those blaspheming beasts think of it, she wondered.

Just then, the Jew shrieked with a piercing howl that Donia did not know humans to be capable of.

"Good!" "Squash his balls!" "Kick his crouch!" "Make sure he never fucks again!" Vulgar shouts from the mob drowned out the man's hysterical cries for help. The sights and sounds stabbed at Donia painfully.

Donia couldn't see Mundek's head anymore. Yes, that was Mundek for sure, she remembered. He was the tailor's son. She recalled Pan Isidor, his father. The tailor's shop wasn't too far from here. It was just around the next corner.

The crowd was thinning; some couldn't take it. She saw Mundek again. Tall Mundek lay on the flagstones of the sidewalk. She heard his moans and groans as those in the center stomped all over him and then there was silence. As the crowd receded from the center, she glimpsed his bashed head. His lanky body, broken and unnaturally twisted, lay sprawling on the bloody stones. She averted her eyes and looked up the street, up the hill abutting the Church of Saint Anthony of Padua. She saw the hill where all the kids went sledding in winter.

But she could not avoid the stench; that was still there. The always neatly dressed and bashful Mundek, who lowered his eyes whenever they met on the street, had emptied his bowels and urinated all over himself. Donia was sick to her stomach and surely would have vomited had she not been distracted by the sight of Edek Edelman, who stood a few feet away from her. Edek stood with his head down, shielding his face with the palms of his hands.

"Edek!" Donia yelled as she approached him. "Edek, it's me, Donia. Edek, are you alright? They didn't—did they? Did they beat you, too?"

Edek turned toward her, raised his head, and dropped his hands. His face was wet and streaked with tears. She stepped toward him and grabbed him by his moist hand, pulling him away from the remaining onlookers. Meekly, he allowed her to lead him back across the street to the gate of their apartment house. Once inside the stairway, he turned toward her and let his head collapse on her shoulder. His body shook and she held him close. Nobody was in the dark hallway to see them both crying.

"Edziu," she said softly, using the diminutive form of Edek that only his parents and grandparents ever used. "Edziu, go up. Your parents must be worrying sick about you. My mama is probably worried about me too. Go up, Edziu. I...I don't know what to say. I am sorry, terribly sorry. I am so shocked."

As Edek started up the steps, Donia's thoughts turned back to the massacred Mundek and she couldn't hold back anymore. Her stomach erupted in a spasm of acidic vomit. Edek stepped down and caressed her hair.

"You are *dobra*—so good, Donia. You are *ladna dziewczynka*. Pretty girl. Pretty girl," he repeated over and over again and then gave her his handkerchief. "I will get rags from our apartment and clean it up. You run up to your mama."

Donia did not run. Unsteadily, slowly, step by step, she reached the third floor. All that time she thought of Edek. As they had held one another, it had occurred to her that he was nearly her same height. His legs stuck out of indecently short Boy Scout-type khaki pants, but his legs were becoming quite muscular. A future footballer, she thought. His face still held childish traces, but he was becoming more attractive, more manly—even with the somewhat long nose.

Surprise of surprises. The nosy Pani Laskawa had not stepped to the window to look outside. She had been so occupied by her mending that she did not witness Mundek's murder. The entire beastly orgy had taken only minutes, yet to Donia it seemed to have lasted an eternity. It took place practically in the shadow of the bell tower of the Church of Saint Anthony of Padua where the Laskawas attended services and where Donia had taken her first communion. Donia wondered whether she would ever again be able to look at the baby Jesus in the arms of Saint Anthony.

Chapter VII. They are Killing Jews

⌒

I left Donia behind me and entered our rooms in "the Stummes' apartment." My parents and my grandparents as well as Cousin Manka and Uncle Joseph comprised the tragic tableau where women sat crying on the beds and men bent over them trying to comfort them.

"They are beating and murdering Jews on the streets again," Uncle Joseph repeated several times.

My father nodded and tapped the night table with clenched fists. My grandfather was murmuring, probably reciting prayers. Both of his hands rested on my grandmother's shoulders.

"I wonder where Heniek is," voiced Manka.

"I sure hope he is all right" my father answered and then, as if just noticing me, "Edek, you were outside. Do you know the man they were beating?"

"No," I lied. "I wasn't there to see, I—"

While I was trying to invent an explanation for my absence, Yanka Stumme opened the door from their rooms and walked in. In one hand, she held a long cigarette holder with a lit cigarette pointing upwards; in the other, she cuddled her customary glass of vodka. Heads turned toward her but nobody said anything; Yanka was in her cups. She sat down next to my mother. Yanka would rarely get out of her night gown, carpet slippers, and *schlafrock*, her bathrobe. She appeared unusually disheveled and truly anesthetized by liquor. Yanka's only contribution to neatness was her hair. Her long, dark, graying hair was laboriously combed and arranged into a pair of pigtails. I often saw her sitting by the mirror in "their" room, brushing and combing her long strands. A vodka glass almost always stood within arm's reach.

Yanka was a large, heavy woman with prominent breasts. She might have been very attractive at one time. Now, when she walked, she sagged. When she sat, she slumped, as if always under a tremendous weight—but of what?

After the war I learned what she feared. Only then did I come to fully understand the reason for her inebriation. Today, as I sit on the couch in this senior residence, I would welcome her presence—cigarette smoke, alcohol odor, and all. As unappetizing as she was then, she would appear delicious to me now. For as old as I am, I am starving for female companionship. Large, broad hipped, with ample breasts, Yanka would do quite well. Those are my feelings now, so many years later, but at that time I felt nothing but disgust for Yanka.

Then, on that day when Jewish blood smeared the sidewalks and courtyards of Lwow, and when Donia embraced me in the hallway and I sobbed bitterly on her shoulder, I felt entirely different sensations: pleasure and thrill. I was excited by the touch of her hard little breasts and the sweet aroma of her hair and neck. Donia became an angel to me. I worshiped her in my dreams as an ethereal being not to be defiled by sensual onslaughts. For sexual relief, I began fantasizing about doing things with Cousin Paula and Aunt Sarah. Yes, I turned fourteen and testosterone invaded me so that I roared with primordial fury.

Celia, the nursing supervisor here at The Blue Ridge Residence, reminds me of Yanka—but only vaguely; only their bodies have the same fullness. Celia's demeanor is highly professional as is her well-ironed and spotless white uniform. Celia never smells of alcohol. She ministers to me with authority yet gentleness. Her friendly smile and tender admonitions sooth me.

"Calm yourself, Doctor Edelman. You mustn't exert yourself so much. It is better that you rest more frequently. Go and sit on the terrace and I will join you there."

"Do you promise, Celia?"

"Yes, we will have iced tea together. Would you like anything sweet to munch on?"

"No, just to talk to you will be sweet enough for me."

"Aha, I see. You are trying your charm on me. I am glad that you are more yourself today."

Celia smiles radiantly and I felt her warmth penetrate my heart.

"But watch your steps as you walk through the hallway. They were going to install another light fixture. It is kind of dark there right now."

Of course, Celia, I think to myself. I look with pleasure to our tête-à-tête and I will be careful. I wouldn't miss the opportunity of being with you.

"Please, Doctor Edelman, pay attention to your walking. You tend to shuffle your feet. Just walk rhythmically, march. One, two. One, two. One, two."

The hallway is lit well enough. I can easily see my feet and the door that leads to the terrace.

"They make such a fuss about everything," I say aloud and remember Celia's instructions to lift my feet.

"One and two, one and two," I repeat. The one and two quickly become "Four plus five, four plus five, four plus five."

Apparently, my brain is better attuned to the cadence of "four plus five" but that does not last. I dredge out the strains from the Polish national anthem that I remember from my childhood. "March, march, Dombrowski," I mutter. I march in rhythm to the stirring martial words all the way to the terrace.

Celia brings a tray with two glasses of tea—hers, well iced; mine without ice. It is good of her to remember that I don't like cold beverages the way most Americans do. There are several brownies on the tray and some napkins too.

"These brownies are homemade. Mrs. Richmond at the reception desk baked these for you."

"That is awfully nice of her." I respond even though I am not fond of sugary desserts.

She sets the tray on a patio side table and sits down next to me.

"You know, Doctor Edelman, I've known you for some time now, but we know so little about one another. Sure, I am familiar with your medical record, but that's about it, and you know nothing about me."

She takes a bite of her brownie and a sip of tea.

"I would like to get acquainted with you," she continues. "Perhaps I don't dare—you probably don't appreciate me being so forward."

She stares at me a moment then takes another drink of tea.

"True, we must maintain our nurse-patient decorum. But I want to tell you that I was once an aspiring writer. In my late teens I thought that I would conquer the world with my romantic novels. What do you think of that?"

She laughs and takes another bite of brownie, them wipes some fallen crumbs off her lap.

"Really, Celia. I would not have suspected it. That is surprising, considering where you are now!"

"Well, maybe I don't look like the exuberant, wild teenager that I once was. Goodness, now I'm a grandma—and pretty heavy, I know."

"I would like to see your work. It would be a nice diversion for me."

"Oh, Doctor Edelman, I think I would be too embarrassed to show it to you. You would think me to be some sex fiend."

"Sex fiend! Now that is something I'd like to read! Bring it. I promise not to share it with anyone. No one else will know about your special talent."

"Well, maybe."

She sets her napkin back on the tray and picks up our two glasses. I have barely touched mine.

"I have to get back to work, Doctor Edelman. Please, be careful as you walk back. Try not to shuffle, okay?"

Celia leaves me and I sit alone for a moment, wondering what juicy manuscripts she might deliver.

I remember to lift my feet carefully as I walk back to my room, humming the rambunctious, naughty tune of "Habanera" from *Carmen*.

Chapter VIII. View from the Attic

As I marched into manhood, it was without the accompaniment of music. I became obsessed with titillating thoughts of sex. Sex drove my being even though all around me the German occupation was becoming ever more brutal. I masturbated whenever I had a semblance of privacy, and sometimes without it. The thrill I obtained from exploring my sensuality was often stifled by a debilitating fear of being caught and deported; or worse, being beaten and maimed.

With every passing week, we heard German and Ukrainian boots more frequently—in our neighborhood, on our sidewalks, in our alleys, courtyards, and stairs. Oh, God, the trampling of boots. One, two. One, two. Sounds of crushing, grinding boots inevitably followed with cries for mercy and screams of pain.

Now they were not only murdering Jews seemingly by whim, but they had begun a systematic door-to-door mass hunt. We were next.

"I heard from reliable sources that a large unit of German soldiers came to Lwow this morning. They must be special because there is a lot of fuss about quartering them."

Pan Burek spoke to my father in a quiet, confidential tone, as he was wont to do when transmitting any news that emerged from his underground Polish contacts. Often he related mere rumors, later proved untrue—and there were plenty of those floating during those troubled times.

Not this time.

"I have facts," Pan Burek said. He was a large man with a round, shaved head and a pleasant, smiling face. Pan Burek, who normally looked like a jolly giant, was grim. His face was stern, exhibiting his deep concern.

"They came from Tarnopol where they removed most of the Jews from their homes and took them away. We know this for a fact. It happened just last week"

It became apparent to me that Pan Burek had ceased to consider me to be a child anymore because this time he did not order me to leave the room. I sat quietly in the antechamber and listened to his hushed voice.

"The rumor is that they are SS commandos who specialize in relocating Jews. Why else would they need all the trucks in town?"

"Yes, I know that they requisitioned all the municipal vehicles for tomorrow. Roman works for the Sanitation Department and he told his mother, Pani Laskawa, about it." My father looked up straight into the eyes of the towering Pan Burek as he confirmed Burek's news.

"What should we do? What can we do? Who can help us?" said my father as he looked around the room, rubbing his hands together nervously. He was normally calm, but his hands trembled and he wrapped his palms together tightly in an unsuccessful attempt to steady them.

"I don't have an inkling what they will do. It may not be as bad as we think. They will probably ship the Jews somewhere to the East. They certainly need workers to rebuild the damaged Russian towns and get their agriculture going again."

Pan Burek forced a smile as he tried to paint the oncoming relocation with an optimistic tinge.

It was difficult for me to tell whether he himself believed what he said because he turned his head away from my father and called in the direction of Pani Cwik, who had just entered the antechamber.

"Here, here, honey," he beckoned to her. "I am talking to Pan Edelman. I will be there in just a minute. Keep the soup warm, darling."

He patted my father on the shoulder, saying, "I really am hoping for the best for you, Kurt."

"Thank you, Panie Burek," my father responded.

Pan Burek left and my father turned to me.

"Edek, go to our rooms and stay with your mother. Don't let her worry unnecessarily. It may not turn out to be so bad. I have something to take care of. I will be back soon."

My father walked out the door of the apartment. He did not go down the stairs, but up toward the third floor. Was he going to Natalia's apartment, to the Laskawys', or to the attic? Certainly he wasn't going to see the elderly woman with cats who lived in the garret. I listened to his footsteps on the stairs, then went to the kitchen in search of my mother.

When he came down, my father was in a less dismal mood, although the news he brought was nothing but ominous.

"I learned that the Ukrainian militia have cancelled leave and everyone has to report for what they are calling 'action' early tomorrow morning, but—"

He began to whisper into my mother's ear. I could not make out much of this secretive talk, but "attic," "action," and "Natalia" were three words that did not escape me.

The next day, "attic," "action," and "Natalia" reverberated in my brain and became the focal point of the drama that unfolded all around me, especially in the courtyards below.

"Get up, Edek. Don't make any noise," my father whispered in my ear as he shook me out of a deep slumber. It was very early in the morning. My mother and father were already dressed—and warmly at that, in spite of it being a sunny fall day. They both carried a satchel, a blanket, and a water bottle.

"Dress quickly and be quiet. We must leave without Pani Yanka or Yacek seeing us. Here, you carry Mother's water bottle. Put on your coat and cap. And there's a knapsack for you."

He pointed to my canvas rucksack that sat at the foot of the bed. The bag was bulging and looked heavy; whatever they had packed inside surely would fall out if not for the leather buckle that secured the flap.

"If they catch us and ship us out, you will need it for the trip."

I slung the heavy bag over my shoulder, asking, "Where will the police take us?"

My father did not reply but merely motioned me to go.

We walked out of our rooms on tiptoes, through the antechamber and out to the staircase. Why was my father leading us up the stairs? Was Natalia going to hide us? So, it was true about my father and Natalia? Those things between my father and Lesia's mother must be true, I thought. Why else would she risk herself by hiding us?

While I was mulling over my father's relationship with Natalia, we reached the third floor and my father put a finger on his lips. He passed by the door to Natalia's apartment and led us up to the attic. He unlocked the iron door. We entered and he locked the door behind us. Nobody had seen us. My father had left a short note on the kitchen table:

Pani Yanka,

We are leaving. We hope to make it to a nearby village and stay with a family that we know there.

Kurt

The musty smell of the attic was still there as I remembered it from before the war but it looked different. Before the war, the attic was partitioned into sections; each assigned to an apartment. It was a place where tenants could store unneeded household items such as unused furniture or suitcases. The wooden partitions and everyone's belongings had since disappeared, the result of anti-fire precautions imposed at the beginning of the war. My parents and I stood in a space just under the roof. There were piles of sand around us; the sand was meant to be used for extinguishing an incendiary bomb, just in case one hit us. My new surroundings: sand piles, a few rusty scraps of bent metal, and a little window at the edge of the attic overlooking the courtyards below.

The courtyards as seen from the little window. I must focus on the courtyards. From that tiny window I could see the courtyard of our apartment house and that of the adjoining building. There was no uniformity to our courtyard. I remember the little grassy areas sectioned off by cement walkways, isolated lilac bushes here and there.

I must force myself to tell about the courtyards because that was where the activity was. No, "activity" is not the word I want. It becomes progressively more difficult for me to select the precise words. Ah, here it is. "Action." I smile, satisfied that I am able to retrieve it from my impaired brain. "The action." "The action" became a sinister term feared by us Jews. As we were about to learn that day, the next, and the days that followed, "action" came to mean the liquidation of a large fragment of the Jewish population in town; an innocent word enough, but one that filled us with terror.

The three of us hidden in the attic were about to face the first—and one of the largest—actions that the Jewish community in Lwow would face. The right place to start would be with us: kneeling at the little window, four stories high.

I want to focus but it is not easy. I am not looking down from the attic but I am looking out the window of my room at the Blue Ridge. At first, I see the trees and the hills, but they get progressively blurry. Not in the way that I experienced the optical migraine before. It is a new sensation that envelopes me. It is as if I am in a fog, detached in a protective cocoon. I am dulled, sensing neither the beauty of the bluish-tinged hills nor the terror to come below. It is not an unpleasant feeling to be above everything in a mental fog. I don't even see clearly my parents as they huddled on their knees next to me and peered cautiously down. Maybe because I am not looking at my parents. They must be terribly scared and I don't want to see their weakness.

"Edek, stay away from the window or somebody may see you," my father whispered and motioned to me to get back.

It strikes me now, here in my room in the nursing home, that in the days of German terror we almost always whispered and often merely motioned with our hands. Enveloped in my fog, I have a sudden urge to hear myself and so I shout "Celia" at the top of my voice. I yell again and again until Celia comes running in.

"Yes, Doctor Edelman? What is the matter? Do you need something?"

"Celia, I want to hear myself." I am curled tightly on my bed, like a child who, frightened by a nightmare, waits for his mother to come pacify him.

"I will never whisper again—not ever. I don't want people to talk in hushed voices. I don't want anyone to be afraid of being heard. It is our right to talk loudly, to shout—to scream if we want to. Well? Isn't it?"

Celia looks at me puzzled, as if I were not Dr. Edelman.

"I am crazy, Celia. I'm sorry. You must think that I am demented. I can't help it. I…Forgive me."

I turn away and stare out the window in my room.

"No, you are not. It is the medicine that dulls you and you are trying to overcome it by yelling out loud. You are trying to penetrate that haze."

How right you are, Celia. I am trying to penetrate that cloudiness, trying to remember what I saw from that little window in the attic that day.

At first I saw an unusual amount of activity among our neighbors as they walked in and out of the house into the street, then back to their apartments. Their seemingly pur- poseless meandering reminded me of actors assuming their positions on a stage before the curtain lifts and the show begins. There was a similar activity in the adjoining apart- ment houses. The street itself was shielded from my view by the wing of a neighboring house. I could not see the approaching police and their vehicles but I sensed their approach from the increasing tempo and excitement among our neighbors in the courtyards.

The brutes entered the courtyard of our building from an adjoining house, followed by a retinue of well-wishers. There were mostly Ukrainian militiamen and a few SS men; ten or so altogether. The Ukrainians had rifles; the Germans came with side arms, canes, and short whips. They paused at the entry to the root cellar. The Ukrainians were immediately surrounded by some of our male neighbors and their groupies from the neighborhood; the Germans stood aloof, surveying our house, though not for long. Pan Fedan, Pan Shoenhoffer, Tadzik, and a few other men approached them.

What would they tell them? That Jews were living here? Would they point to our apartment windows on the second floor? Perhaps they had heard us go up the stairs to the attic and had heard the iron door squeak. Would they gesture toward the attic? My heart pounded as I watched the Germans listen and nod their heads. I was very scared. Fear overwhelmed me and I began to sweat.

Then, as if on cue, the chorus entered the scene. Women in their Sunday dresses appeared—the most prominent being Natalia!—and served the men refreshments. Thank God, Donia was not one of them. The serious, often sad Natalia became the life of the party, for party it indeed became. I can still see Natalia as she held a tray of little cups and flitted from one group to the other, her peasant skirt whirling around her hips. She bowed graciously to the SS men, coming quite near them as they reached for the libations. The SS men began to relax. They exchanged words with her and she laughed with them. She was outwardly forward with the Ukrainian militiamen, touching them, perhaps flirting. One or two pulled her toward them and embraced her. Men patted each other on the back. They were a party of monsters, and Natalia kept them spirited.

"I always knew she was a false hussy. Look how she caters to them," my mother broke the prolonged silence. Her comment was almost inaudible and sounded more like a hiss.

"Sha, sha," my father responded soothingly.

I turned toward him and saw a smile briefly enliven his face.

Fifteen minutes of joyful fellowship and the beasts left, but not before two militiamen descended into the root cellar to search it. They found nobody there. But they found my grandparents in their one-room apartment on the ground floor of the adjoining house.

My grandmother was the first to be shoved into the courtyard. I still see her clearly, dressed in black from head to toes: black scarf, black sweater, black skirt, black stockings and black shoes. The white bundle—it was a bulging pillowcase—that she carried in her arms offset the blackness. They jeered at her and pushed her around, trying to grab the bundle from her, but she held onto it for dear life. The food and clothing in it meant survival in the place where she believed that they were going to be resettled.

Then they shoved my grandfather outside. Seeing his wife so molested, he approached one of the Germans and began to plead with him. The monster whipped my grandfather across his face and kicked him in the crotch. My grandfather bent forward, doubled over in pain.

My father gasped and rose, running toward the attic door.

"Don't go, Kurt! Don't go," pleaded my mother. "You will not be able to help them."

She ran after him, grabbing the sleeve of his coat with her good hand and touching his back gently with the little stumps of her left hand.

"Don't go. They will take you also and we will lose you. You will not be able to help them. You have a son and a wife; we will be destroyed without you," she tried to reason with him. "You love us too, don't you?" she added quietly.

My father stopped at the door, turned around and put his hands around my mother but turned his face toward me. The torment raging inside of him was painted on his face and tears were streaming down his cheeks. He was a good son and the pain he was suffering was breaking him. He collapsed to his knees, clutched my mother, and sobbed quietly.

Tears force themselves out of my old eyes as I write these words. However, I am not the only one affected. I suddenly notice that Celia and Ginny are sitting at my bedside. Their eyes are moist. Why didn't I notice them when they came in?

"Why are you crying?" I ask them.

"It's your father. It must have been devastating to watch his elderly parents get beaten and abused. I love my parents and it would be a tragedy for…Not to be able to help your parents, what a torture that would be!"

"Celia, how did you know about my father?"

"You read it to us. Don't you remember Doctor Edelman? Just now you—No matter."

"We will help you to the bathroom and will be back a bit later," adds Ginny.

"Did I tell you about my father?" I ask.

The haze I am in is evaporating very slowly. My ability to recollect returns, at least somewhat. I focus my gaze on Celia and Ginny and they know that I have come back from the past. I want to tell them how appreciative I am for their compassion but cannot find the words. I can still write, but it is ever more difficult to express myself with spoken words.

"Are you finished, Doctor Edelman?"

"No, of course not. I still have to tell about Natalia's and Donia's deaths."

"Are you finished on the potty? We will help you back to bed."

"How did you know about my father, Celia?"

"Ginny, flush the toilet, please. Let's take Doc Edelman back to bed. He seems to be responsive now."

I am so embarrassed for not realizing that I was sitting on the toilet and talking to those young women as if we were having cocktails in the parlor. My embarrassment doesn't seem to faze them in the least.

"Doctor Edelman, what happened to your grandparents? Where were they taken?"

"What can I tell you, Ginny? They, along with many thousands of other Jews from Lwow, never left the town. All of them were massacred in the local cemetery and at other locations on the outskirts. At first, women had to give up their jewelry. Then they all were forced to undress and then…"

"They were butchered!" interjects Celia.

"Yes, ultimately." I take a deep breath, then sigh. I turn my body and look at the window. "Many fell into the ravines, merely wounded. Some, especially children, were not even nicked. They were buried alive and died slowly under other bodies."

"I never thought that humans were capable of such heinous deeds," says Ginny.

My caretakers are quiet for a moment. Ginny breaks the silence.

"What about Natalia? What happened to her? She probably saved your lives."

Yes, Ginny, I think to myself. You are right. I believe that after the beasts left our courtyard, I saw Natalia look up at the attic window and smile. Oh Ginny, if I only knew what happened to her.

"I am sure that she died a natural death after the

war—probably somewhere in Austria. You see, later, many Ukrainians fled from Lwow when the Soviet Army began to defeat the Germans and were coming closer to us."

I like to think that when my father visited Europe after my mother died in America, that my father saw Natalia wherever she took refuge and helped her. I also like to think that the bullets that pierced my grandparents' skin killed them instantaneously as they held each other while reciting the Shema, the ancient watchword of Judaism: *Hear, O Israel, the Lord our God, the Lord is One.*

+ + + + + + + + +

The big "action" was over in two days and the Death Commandos departed for another area. Rumors circulated that some of those rounded-up Jews had been transported eastward to settle the former Soviet territories. The remaining Jews in town paid vast amounts to Ukrainian men for travel to the East to find the "relocated" members of their families and to bring them aid.

The cruel and perfidious behavior of those who accepted that money cannot be described. They, like most of the non-Jewish residents, knew that tens of thousands of Jews had been murdered in town or somewhere nearby. And yet, some fueled the hopes of those surviving relatives. The unscrupulous vultures must have had a good laugh at the expense of the duped Jews as they fed upon their hopes and grief.

Some surviving Jews deluded themselves that the Nazis had satisfied their bloodthirstiness. Those who did—and even those who didn't—mourned and carried on. My parents and I re-entered the Stummes' apartment, demolished in spirit but determined to persevere another day. America was our hope. America might yet enter the war.

Chapter IX. December, 1941

"Edek, leave Yacek alone. It's getting late. You should be on the mattress and asleep," my father called from our bedroom.

"Coming, Father. Five more minutes! Pani Yanka doesn't mind," I yelled back from Stumme's rooms.

I was in the process of reshaping my nose by pressing it upward against the warm tiles of Stumme's stove. I believed that this treatment would stop my nose from growing longer and that hopefully, I would look less Semitic. Besides, that room was the only warm place in our apartment during that bitterly cold December of 1941.

Even before the war it was difficult to keep all of our rooms warm in winter. Generally, we maintained a fire in two bedroom ceramic stoves. It was pleasant to come in from outside and warm yourself standing against those tall stoves or to play in the kitchen next to the cooking stove and sniff the meat as it stewed in a rich sauce seasoned with paprika.

Winters before the war bring other pleasant memories to my mind but also some frightening ones. I remember how I used to ice skate in the hospital yard across the street. They turned it into a skating rink by simply dousing the flat yard with water and letting it freeze. I glided between Roman and Donia, holding onto their hands as they steered through the multitude of other skaters. On those occasions my heart overflowed with joy and pride by being so catered to by older kids, especially since they were non-Jewish.

But there was literally the other side of the street—my side. We lived a few houses down the block from the Church of Saint Anthony. Behind the church there was a steep street, a popular sledding site. I had a single-person sled that the kids derided as a "baby crib." Nastier kids would gang up on me and sometimes overturn me, shouting derogatory names at me as I tumbled down the hill.

"Stinking Jew-boy! Dirty Jew baby!" they yelled.

But their favorite slur was a ditty: "Oh, you Jewish swine go to Palestine," which happens to rhyme in Polish also. When my father walked by though, torment ceased. He was either feared or respected. I'm not sure which one—maybe it was both.

"Doctor Edelman, here we are. Did you have a chance to produce a sample?" A nurse intrudes upon my keying.

"Oh, it's you. No, not yet." I brusquely acknowledge her presence.

"You can do it now. Sit on the edge of the bed. I will prop you up with a pillow. Here is the bottle. I will be back in a minute."

The act of inserting one's penis into the neck of a streamlined bottle while sitting is degrading; less so when standing. Somehow, urinating in an erect position is a natural act for a male. But I am weak, without much strength to hold the bottle with one hand while trying to keep myself from falling with the other. My eyesight is affected and it is difficult to maintain balance.

How ironic! When I was a boy, urinating was rather fun,

especially outdoors and particularly during winter when there was fresh snow on the ground. We had contests: Who could squirt the farthest? Who had enough pee to write his name in the snow in one swoop? The yellow etchings in the white snow lasted until the sun would obliterate them and then we hoped for another snowfall, venturesome, competitive and curious as we were. What a dramatic physiological change from those days! No pressure now, no stream. The best I can do is to direct the dripping and hope to prevent soaking my underwear. My bladder no longer has the capacity of youth.

We weren't bashful then, and so I learned that my penis was like the penis of any other Jewish boy just not as thick as that of gentile friends. Our penises were circumcised, sleeker, more manageable. Their penises were…

"I am back, Doctor Edelman. I see you did your duty. Please give me your arm. We will see whether your blood pressure behaves."

Of course I obey. She means well; they all mean well. They—the staff and the drugs—keep me alive, and thus far, relatively comfortable. It is winter now in the Blue Ridges and not as severe as in 1941. It was unseasonably cold on the eighth or ninth of December. Which day was it? In any case, right after the Japanese attacked Pearl Harbor. Pan Burek had come over, bubbling with joy.

"America is at war. America is at war," he kept repeating to us and to Pani Yanka. "Of course, the local rag is claiming a big victory for Japan against the American fleet, but that's the propaganda. They are lying as usual."

"I heard that the Soviets stopped the German Army in front of Moscow," my father said in a quiet voice.

"Yes, yes. Erich wrote to me that…he will need more

warm socks for the winter. Which means that…they don't think they will conquer Russia…any time soon…They are hoping for spring," blurted Yanka Stumme between puffs of cigarette smoke as she shuffled around the kitchen, then checked again on the draft of frigid air passing through cracks under the balcony door.

"Panie Edelman, please come here!" she called to my father. "Look, the water pipes are coated with ice in the kitchen. I can actually see icicles forming."

"Yes, Pani Stumme, I saw them. The water in the pipes will freeze unless something is done about the insulation."

My father answered politely, but he intimated using carefully chosen words that the Stummes were now the owners of the apartment.

Nothing was done about the draft. The temperature outside dipped lower and the water in the exposed kitchen pipes froze. No running water. But our elation to America's entry into the war was not chilled by the bitter winter. In fact, Pan Burek confirmed that trains of frozen German soldiers were being evacuated from the Moscow front.

"All the better. With America fighting the Germans, our tragedy will be over. All we need is to survive a few more months," I overheard my father comforting my mother. "It is a ghastly fate that Grandma and Grandpa Edelman and so many others were taken. I wish they could be here to see this day—this day of hope," continued my father. "But, there are still Romka, Sarah, and Heniek—they weren't taken. I will try to invite them over so that we can rejoice together. Perhaps they will be able to come," my father speculated.

And so, icicles on the water pipes notwithstanding, six of them came: five relatives plus David Dauman, all gathered in the kitchen. The adults embraced affectionately and most cried. Everyone brought a bit of food and a small or partially filled bottle of spirits, except for Dauman. He brought an unopened bottle of champagne, a loaf of warm, crusty rye bread and a package of fresh cold cuts. I was salivating, but first the toasts.

"May we live to witness the annihilation of Nazis," proposed my father.

Up went the little glasses with vodka and down the throats went the fiery liquor. Then Heniek toasted and we all downed the vodka, including me. Finally, they reached for the bread and meat; I was the first to grab. Dauman raised his glass and the others followed, including me. I overheard snippets of optimistic conversation. Faces, reddened by alcohol, began to relax. I even noticed a smile appear on my father's face—the first one I'd seen since our return from the attic.

Sarah and Dauman were the most affected by the merriment. I saw them exchange lustful looks and hold hands under the table. Aunt Sarah (her husband Zygmunt, if he was still alive, was somewhere with the Red Army) was stroking David's lap. He was amply reciprocating under the table with his other hand. Dauman was a refugee from western Poland. His wife and child had probably already been deported to Tremblinka for slaughter. This was a party of condemned— those still there were desperate to enjoy figments of life. They lived with a knowledge that they would be murdered unless the Allies defeated Hitler and his brutal minions soon, and they dared to hope.

"They will take care of me. The *Wehrmacht* will protect me," boasted Dauman loudly.

He was an artist, a portrait painter whom the German officers housed in their quarters. He was fed well and protected—so far. He painted their likenesses, which they sent to their proud families. He painted many of the Junker caste and it would not be unreasonable to think that all those portraits, paid for by the cold cuts I ate and the champagne we drank, disappeared. No, I am sure not. Many must still exist. In how many houses, above how many mantelpieces, in present-day Germany hang ancestors decorated in military regalia painted by David Dauman, the Polish Jew who gained the affection (and more) of my aunt Sarah?

Whether he deserved Aunt Sarah's intimacy or not, I don't know. But I do know that he was one of the most famous portraitists in Europe, at least according to what he told us that afternoon. Dauman regaled us with stories from his days as an art student in Paris. I was all ears when he described the nude artists' balls—I mean balls where men and women danced together, adorned only with a big fig leaf. Boozed-up as I was, it was easy for me to fantasize pretty women, all naked except between their legs. I had never seen a really naked woman except years earlier when I visited Cousin Paula. She didn't mind putting on her undergarments in my presence. Paula probably thought that I was too young to notice.

As for naked men, no problem. I had seen my father mostly naked, and my boy playmates naked where it counted. But looking then at the short, dumpy Dauman, I couldn't imagine who would want to look at his flabby naked body with just a leaf to cover his essentials, much less to dance with him. Yet Aunt Sarah must have held him naked in her arms, and she was a fairly good woman to look at. Still nurturing my crush on Aunt Sarah, I imagined her in the act of disrobing and attaching a fig leaf to her pubic area. But how? What did she pin it to?

"Was it a large leaf? Didn't it fall off with dancing?" I was emboldened to ask aloud.

No one answered. It must have been a toga and not a leaf at all, I reasoned with myself. Just then, Heniek took the proceedings out of Dauman's hands and proposed a toast.

"To Paris! To France! To the days of youth and gaiety!"

"To Paris! Drink with cognac!" All intoned and we imbibed again.

"That's right, Heniek studied medicine in France," said Aunt Sarah, looking down at me where I sat on the floor for lack of anywhere else to sit. "A Jew couldn't have studied in Poland. Those bastards EN-DEKS, Polish fascists, they would beat you to death here at Lwow University. Here, in your Poland. Learn, Edek, you who likes the Poles so much."

"Yes, I was probably in France at the same time as Dauman," Heniek interjected, trying to change the subject away from Poles. He glanced at Pani Yanka as she slipped into the kitchen and squatted on the floor next to me with her own supply of alcohol in one hand and a cigarette holder in the other.

I thought that it was good of her to permit all of us to get together in "her" kitchen, but I was astonished because she seemed to be like one of us—Jewish.

"Last time I traveled to France on a motorcycle," continued Heniek, relating funny incidents about his travels through Germany in the mid-thirties, "the Germans didn't bother me since it was still three years before the war. They even treat me leniently now since they need me. I am the camp physician in Brzuchowice. Even the SS guards come to me for medical advice. They have problems with venereal diseases, as you can imagine. They are men, right?"

Here, an inebriated Heniek looked at my father and giggled, then suddenly stopped and became deadly serious. "They assure me that if they liquidate the camp they will save me."

All of us knew what the word "liquidate" implied. The jovial atmosphere was gone. Everybody became silent, given to their private fears; the party had ended. Dauman squeezed Sarah's hand tightly and pulled her up from the chair. They left without a word and the rest followed. My mother and Pani Yanka disappeared into their respective bedrooms. Only Heniek lingered in the kitchen for a few minutes, talking with my father. He seemed absolutely sober.

"You know, Kurt, our only hope is America. The war must end soon or they will slaughter us all."

"America is powerful. If they concentrate on Germany, the war will be over within six months. Now that the Soviets are transferring their Siberian armies from Asia, Hitler may be defeated even sooner."

Heniek nodded, while my father approached him closely and continued in a whisper.

"You know of Natalia, my Ukrainian woman-friend? You gave me some condoms then. Have I told you what she told me?" my father said softly into Heniek's ear. I strained to hear the rest but the alcohol and the excitement of the evening had become too much for me. I quickly opened the door to the balcony, felt the rush of frigid air, hung my head over the railing and let all the bread and sausages flush out.

Six months passed and Germany was doing well. America was not strong in 1941. During that half-year while America geared up for war and the Soviets sacrificed their millions, Sarah, Dauman, Heniek, and the rest of my relatives were well on the way to becoming decaying corpses in the many ravines and pits of the local parks and cemeteries. Dauman's German clients could not—or would not—protect him. Heniek's SS patients indeed warned him and let him escape from their camp, but others caught him wandering the streets without a place to hide and executed him on the spot.

Only my mother, my father, and I survived to face yet another more terrible stage: The Ghetto. Pani Yanka turned out to be our loyal sympathizer and helper. My father's Ukrainian woman-friend had remained an enigma thus far. Natalia Fedan lived on the third floor. She was Lesia's mother. My father and Lesia's mother? How could that be? Besides, there were other Natalias in the neighborhood and in town.

Another visit by my nurse. I actually like Celia. To be sure, she is fat—practically obese—but her behind still retains the proper contours and inspires my imagination. Aunt Sarah also had a nice shape and I am sure that Dauman enjoyed that. As for Sarah, Dauman offered her companionship and food, and relieved her loneliness and fear; perhaps she did enjoy his caresses.

I know what it is now to be lonely and to have sex only vicariously. To imagine. To fantasize. Still more, to hope. Perhaps for Celia?

"Doctor Edelman!" Celia really enunciated the "doctor." "Your laptop was on the floor. You have to be careful. I know it's hard for you. I will come back during my lunch hour to help. I can type for you."

I know that she is right. I must preserve all those words much more than my life, which, in any case, is oozing away.

I like to think that David Dauman and Aunt Sarah died embracing each other. I like to think that Pani Ala and

Tusiek also died in each others arms. Oh, I haven't told about them yet.

"Celia!"

"Yes, Doctor Edelman?"

"Will you please hold my hand when I die?"

"Yes, Doctor Edelman."

Chapter X. In the Dentist's Chair

Tusiek + Ala

Pani Laskawa tried to keep her daughter from going out on the street too often and from straying too far. She feared that they would catch young Donia in one of the round-ups and send her away to Germany as slave labor. To the occupiers, that was all any Pole was good for—slaves for Tadzik and his super race! Poles were allowed to go only to elementary school for fear that further education would turn them into leaders; an enslaved nation doesn't need leaders. Some Polish physicians, lawyers, and teachers had already disappeared.

Donia's brother Roman was lucky. He got a job with the town sanitation department. He walked far to work every day and the work was dirty, but at least he could get out of the house. He had an identification card, a *Kennkarte*, with a big letter P on it that stood for "Pole." It was definitely better than being a Jew. The Jewish ID was a band with a blue Star of David on a white field worn on the right arm. Those poor Edelmans, thought Donia. They were cowering in the Stummes' apartment, seldom leaving it. But so were doctor-dentist Pani Ala and her dental technician, Tusiek. The two of them worked and lived together in the apartment a floor below her and her mother.

Donia often wondered why it was that she had empathy for Jews and for people like Pani Ala who was close friends with the Jew Tusiek. Donia was very fond of Dr. Ala. She admired her beautiful face that was enveloped in long brown hair, and her green eyes so full of care and understanding that, just by looking at you during an examination, the pain in your mouth diminished. When Dr. Ala talked to Donia, the girl felt soothing drops of balm on her face. Dr. Ala was crippled and her right leg dragged as she struggled to walk. How tragic, thought Donia. When the dentist performed an examination or drilled teeth, her large body leaned on her good leg, but mostly she sat on a high stool next to her patients.

"Pani Doctor, should I bring my head closer to you?" Donia asked when she saw that Pani Doctor Ala strained to use the dental mirror to see her aching gums.

"No child, I will be fine. Just…I will sit for a minute. But it is awfully nice of you to be concerned." Pani Ala smiled warmly, showing her perfect white teeth. Donia saw the face of an attractive forty-year-old woman with full, beautifully shaped lips such as she saw in pictures of American movie queens.

While Pani Ala was resting, Donia was tempted to ask her about her leg. Was she perhaps crippled by polio? She held back her question though. Donia knew that such a question would have been improper and impolite coming from a fifteen-year-old girl. She had to be content to simply be near such a lovely person. Donia thought about Pan Tusiek, fortunate Pan Tusiek. He was a lucky Jew.

Donia was a frequent visitor to Dr. Ala's apartment. She liked to be in her presence, but there were other reasons too, like curiosity and the occasional toothache. Genteel Pan Tusiek was there at all times, to be sure. But he was small in stature and seldom talked. He was the kind of person one didn't notice, especially next to large Pani Ala and their boisterous friends who used to visit them before the German occupation.

The relationship between Pani Ala and Pan Tusiek had excited Donia's curiosity long before the war. They were so different from each other and yet they lived in harmony. The Laskawas did not ever hear them quarrel nor did they see any signs of familiarity between them. That was amazing, considering that there was only one bedroom with one large bed in their apartment. Their friends were unusual to say the least: two lean women who dressed in men's jackets and riding boots and a tall thin man with long hair who wore a fedora. On Sunday afternoons when the weather was good, they would all sit on the kitchen balcony and consulted racing forms or wrote down their bets on little chits of paper.

"Look at them, Donia." Pani Laskawa would point below to their balcony.

"They are betting on horses. The odd-looking man must be a bookie, and Lord knows what else he does. Those women belong to the racy clique, that's obvious. And these two dress like men." In a derisive tone, Pani Laskawa continued her assessment of Pani Ala's visitors.

Just then, Pani Ala reached out to one of the women and took her hand in hers, patting it and laughing loudly.

"I bet you there is more between them all than meets the eye. It is not enough for Ala to live with a Jew and not go church—their friends are very peculiar. That's what you get whenever there is a Jew in a pile."

"But, Mama," Donia remonstrated. "You like Pan Tusiek and the Edelmans."

"Yes, yes. You are right. Our neighbors are good people, but Jews should keep to themselves. There is a lot of mixing these days…religious intermarriages and other goings on.

I've noticed that Kurt Edelman is paying special attention to Natalia Fedan from across the hall."

"Oh, Mama, they just talk. Don't be so suspicious. Pan Edelman also stops to chat with you and you don't seem to mind it."

"Make sure, Donia, that you find an honest, practicing Catholic man for a husband."

With that instruction for her daughter's future, Pani Laskawa concluded their discourse on Pani Ala, her Jewish assistant, and their visitors, but she could see that her daughter did not cease to think about them. Donia was intrigued that such a diverse group could be so friendly with one another merely because of a shared interest in horses. There must be something more, she thought. But what?

Two years into the German occupation, the Laskawas would learn that there was nothing more except an intense love and admiration between two professionals—a lovely, but crippled, woman and a kind, gentle man.

But it was earlier, just after Stumme took over the Edelman's apartment, as the evening approached, that Donia let herself into Ala's kitchen from the ground-level balcony.

"Pani Doctor, Pani Doctor, it is me, Donia. I want you to look at my tooth," she announced in a quiet voice. She always walked in without ceremony so there was nothing unusual about her entry.

"Are you here?" Donia asked but was met with silence, except for sounds of sobbing coming from the bedroom. Curiosity possessed her and she tiptoed closer and sat down in the dentist's chair. She was surrounded by semi-darkness. The door that opened from the examination room to the bedroom was ajar and she could see Ala and Tusiek in the light of two softly flickering candles. Pani Ala lay on an unmade bed. Tusiek knelt beside the bed, massaging the toes, ankle, and calf of her withered leg. Neither had taken off the white lab coat that each of them always wore when they treated patients. The forearm of her right arm partly covered her face. She repeated his name through tears that she struggled to hold back.

"Tusiek, Tusiek, my sweet Tusiek, my darling. I will not live without you. My brother will hide you. But if the Germans take you, I will go with you. When they take us, we will die together in one another's arms."

Pani Ala turned and faced Pan Tusiek, stretching her hands to him. He shoved the contraption of metal and leather that she used as a brace off the bed. She grasped him and pulled him on top of herself in a tight embrace. His head rested on her breast and she began to rub his back with tender strokes.

"Tusiek, darling. I love you. Please, let's hold each other."

Her chin touched his balding head and she began to kiss it while he passionately kissed her breasts, now partly uncovered. Although she was much larger than he, both lying thus, the difference was not so evident. Tusiek's lab coat settled above Pani Ala's; from the whiteness of the merged coats, they appeared as one.

Pani Ala stopped crying.

"Tusiek, I want you to be with me always. Let's swear that we will live or die together."

Tusiek answered with his hand, placing it under Ala's smock and caressing the calf of her good leg.

It was time for Donia to depart. Fortunately, the couple was so engrossed in one another that they never glanced toward the examination room. Quietly, Donia stepped down from the dentist's chair and left the same way she had entered. It was dark out in the stairwell. She looked back toward their bedroom but there was no gleam of light. They had extinguished the candles. Theirs is a love that I want, she thought. Deep affection, admiration, lust. Would the honest, Catholic man that her mother wished for her provide her with such love? Donia hoped.

Chapter XI. In and Out of the Cage

Then there was the Ghetto and that was hell on earth. The remaining fifteen thousand of us—from a Jewish population that was once one hundred thousand strong—were shut in a cage. We—my father, my mother, and I—were among these "lucky" ones. We were lucky indeed.

A few days before we were forced to walk into the cage, German and Ukrainian police entered "Stumme's apartment" despite the German eagle with the swastika in its talons that guarded the door. Somebody must have informed the police that we lived there. They knew Mother and I were there. They knew in which two rooms we lived because they barged directly into our room from the antechamber, leaving "Stumme's rooms" alone, and Yanka and Yacek unmolested.

The German policemen, two large *Schutzpolizei*, strode toward my mother and me. They grabbed us and shoved us mightily against the windowsill. Stunned and bruised by the impact, I plopped on the floor. My mother gasped, then collapsed next to me. Father was not with us at the time; he might have been working on a roof somewhere.

How my mother suffered the ordeal, I don't know; I never looked at her lying next to me. I simply did not want to see or hear my mother in distress. She might have been hurt, bleeding, unconscious, crying hysterically, or moaning pitifully—I don't know. I do know that she would have tried to conceal her maimed left hand. She always hid it from view; it was such a source of embarrassment to her. I also know that in an indescribable fear, I wet my shorts and legs, and was lying in a puddle of urine. But I kept my eyes open and observed how the Ukrainian police ransacked our two little rooms, taking any items of value and depositing them on the table. Those would be taken away. We, too, were going to be taken away to a ravine, to be massacred like all those Jews before us.

But, no! One of the German policemen picked up some photographs that had fallen out of a family album during the ransacking. He stopped when he noticed a picture of my father. He studied it for a few moments, then eyed me with a penetrating glance.

"That is my father! That is my father!" I managed to whimper.

Then he looked at my mother who was probably begging him to spare us. Since I mentally blocked out my mother's presence during that entire episode, I am not sure what she did. That policeman looked at me again and beckoned the other *Schutzpolizei* toward the door. They both departed our room, leaving us on the floor. The Ukrainians took their loot and followed their German masters.

The photo showed my father as a military officer. He was wearing a Polish Army uniform. The picture must have been taken during a gala occasion because my father wore a saber on his belt and his riding boots were polished so that they reflected the light. I am sure that the German police-man was a Polish citizen prior to World War II and had most likely also served in the Polish Army. To him, it could have been a case of professional courtesy, possibly a whim. To me, it was a miracle.

I met Donia the next day by chance in the stairwell of the first floor landing.

"It was Tadzik who denounced you! It must have been Tadzik who ratted," said Donia.

"Are you sure?" I gripped the banister hard.

"Yes, I saw him!" She stamped her foot. "He showed them where you lived. He was so smug when their police vehicle stopped by our gate. He was on the sidewalk and talked to them. You don't know how happy I was when I saw those Germans and Ukrainians walk out of your apartment without taking you! They already had Jews on the truck in front of our house. They had to sit with their hands up on the bed of the truck and those beasts were hitting them. I am so thankful that it wasn't you and your parents on that truck."

Her words were full of concern; my heart overflowed with gratitude—and more. I wanted to express my love for her but I could only think of the Edek who urinated all over himself out of fear. Did this Edek have the courage to reveal his pent up love? No.

A day or so later, I met Donia again. It was on that day before we left the "Stummes' apartment"—our house, the house where I was born. It was one day before, without a farewell glance at the house, we walked off into the cage.

"Thank you, Donia. You are such a very good girl. So *dobra*. I…" I bravely began while Donia again dwelled on our luck at avoiding the *selekcja*, selection for death.

"I am happy that you are alive. I saw even Bolek breathe with relief when we saw them leave you and your mom alone. He is not like his brother Tadzik, that hater."

On that last day, as Donia empathized with me while we stood on the steps of the dark staircase, I think that I saw tears glistening on her cheeks.

"Good luck, Edziu. And good luck to your parents. I am so terribly sorry to see you leave. I will pray for you but I am not sure whether prayers do anything."

Looking at Donia's feet, for I could not force myself to look at her lovely dark eyes, I was in the grip of a powerful feeling: my first love. I was still disgusted with myself for wetting my pants and all I could manage to say was, "You are such a good and pretty girl."

As she extended her arms to embrace me, I bashfully stepped back, changing my focus from her feet to my own. I continued to murmur under my nose, "You are such a good and pretty girl," as if these were the only words I was capable of uttering.

"Edek, you are a fine young man. You will be a great footballer," she responded and, recognizing my consternation, changed the subject. "We are also leaving the apartment. My mama told me that we will be better off away from here, away from the Ukrainians who hate us...us, Polish people...away from Lwow. We will go to stay with my father's family in Krakow where we will be safer."

Impulsively, without another word, I turned around and ran upstairs, sobbing. Although I am trying, I don't remember how, if at all, we said our final goodbyes to our former neighbors. I'm sure that the farewell to those neighbors who were friendly to us was heart-wrenching.

Actually, I am having a bad day today. The optical migraine clouds not only my vision but also dissolves my memory, and there is pain.

"Celia, Celia are you there?" Of course not. I better use the buzzer. I hope Celia is on duty.

"Please give me extra-strength Tylenol. It usually helps. Thank you."

"Yes, Doctor Edelman. I am Ginny, not Celia…but I can help you."

The tablets will help.

"Thank you, Ginny. Yes, you are helping me."

I can see myself and my parents on that extremely hot August of 1942 as we furtively walked toward the blocks of tenement houses designated as the Ghetto. We only carried medium-sized paper bags and in them the precious few possessions we wanted to safeguard. We wanted to appear inconspicuous, not as Jews leaving our dwelling place for the last time. All the local bandits and opportunists who wanted to enrich themselves would stop Jews, beat them, rob them, and often brutally torture and murder them. It was like walking the gauntlet, especially under the railroad bridge which was one of the entries into the designated cluster of Ghetto apartment houses. We were lucky. We made it and entered the cage. Another miracle?

The pictures from the cage assail me. They strike me like projectiles fired at my head from all directions. My poor head. I see the living skeletons of three filthy, smelly children, all younger than me. These orphans with smudged faces and tangled long hair scratch their heads vigorously. They cease only long enough to point at me and beg for food.

It would indeed be a miracle if I were able to finish my story. I am desperately trying to placate the wretched brood.

"Wait, wait. They will be serving dinner soon. I will be glad to share it with you, but first you must wash. The staff will not let you visit with me. You smell like that sewage on our balcony. Remember how we used to shit and piss on the balconies and the staircase of that decrepit building because there was no water to flush the toilets? Remember? How could you forget?"

Edek, you stank too. Edek, Edek, Edek. You stank as bad as we did, but your Mom did give us a morsel of food occasionally, even though we didn't wash or change our clothes for weeks. How you stank too, Edziu. Edziu, you stank. You, too, had lice in your filthy hair, Edziu. Edziu, you stank. Every "Edziu" they fling at me painfully reverberates in my skull, ever quieter as the Tylenol takes effect. But then, a loud swish and forty ropes begin to swing.

Jewish men swing with nooses around their necks from every balcony on our block. They do not sway in unison. Rather, it is a random sort of swaying. Actually it is the boots and naked feet that sway, urine and shit dripping from them, splashing the sidewalk below. My God, I am being splashed!

"You dirty, perverted Jewish swine, keep moving! Keep walking, right underneath them. We will make sure that you see every bit of their ugly strangled bodies. You little filthy Jew, keep moving with the others, I say! Keep moving…see how we do it…you will be the next…you smelly little Jewish curd, keep moving!"

From every corner of the cage, SS men aim their bayonets at my head and the stabs hurt. "Keep moving, you little Jewish curd…keep moving, you little Jewish piece of shit."

"Don't prod me with your bayonets. Not at my head…my head hurts. Ginny, how it hurts! Ginny, I must have another tablet. The ones you gave me don't work."

"Doctor Edelman, it is I, Celia. Ginny went off duty three hours ago. You must have dozed off. No matter. I will give you another—better medicine."

"Thank you, Celia."

"It should help your headache."

"Yes, I am having these debilitating nightmares. It is hard for me to shake them off."

"I am afraid, Doctor Edelman, that you will have to see the neurologist again. I will make an appointment for you."

"Yes, my head pains me more than ever."

"Perhaps you should let your mind rest and stop writing this book—at least for a while."

I value your concern and advice, dear Celia, but I must return to the cage so that I can spring free from it—completely free. Free for eternity. I will be free when this tale of the nine of us is finally told.

To me, there are two life-saving holes in the cage. The first hole is a guarded gate to the Ghetto. I know that this hole will eventually be my salvation because my father marches through this hole very early in the morning, and wearily marches back into the cage every evening. Father and the other specially selected Jews are the Ghetto work detail. Conceivably, I could march out with them, unchallenged by the guards. But where would I march to? Who would help me? Who would hide me?

The Jews muster in front of the Ghetto gate. When the gate is opened, they march out, carefully screened by the guards, and are forced to sing happy drinking songs. Then, still under guard, they break up the rocks. Hours later, they march yet again under guard to the cage, forced anew to make merry; this time they recite vulgar ditties. If anyone stumbles or falls, he is separated from the formation at the hole and they execute him on the spot.

It is Kurt through the hole, out and in; Kurt through the hole, out and in. In and out; out and in. Or is it in, then out? No matter, it adds up to one hundred and twenty days: three months. Everyday it hurts. My head hurts more and more.

The second hole that saves my life is a hole in the ground right next to the building where we sleep. My father dug that hole and covered it with rusty sheet metal. The hole is narrow but deep—just large enough for my mother to slide down and sit on a stoop of clay. For me, there is only a place on her lap; my head touches the sheet metal. Whenever rumor circulates that the next day they will be hunting for Jews, very early in the morning my mom and I scramble down into the hole while Father covers us up and walks toward the gate to be counted and marched off to the rock pile. My mother and I sit for hours in the hole waiting for my father to return from work and to release us. We sit those hours in fear and in muck. A boy on his mother's lap. After all, we are human and subject to biological needs. What price, survival?

Then, in the fall of 1942, squalor and fear became unbearable. The urge to survive enflamed me. I wanted to live; I wanted to get out no matter what.

"Did Pani Helena leave you any message about me, Father?" I asked him when the others who lived in our room—including those three filthy orphans—quieted down for the night. It appeared that only my parents and I were still tossing on our mattresses.

"No, I would have told you. The only thing I found under the stone was that little bit of bread and lard that you ate just a while ago," my father replied, irritated.

"Tomorrow, if you can, leave another note, Kurt. We must save Edek," my mother implored my father.

"I will, if they send us to work at the same quarry. Otherwise…"

When Pani Helena finally let my father know that she would be willing to hide me in her apartment outside of the

Ghetto, I welcomed the opportunity without much introspection and despite the risk of death that I would face when breaking out of the cage. Then also, there was Donia to dream about; now there is only her memory. I had to risk life in order to gain life.

Now, so many years later, I face the same risky choice. What if my neurologist recommends brain surgery? Will I be willing to take that risk to postpone my death a little longer? Just a little longer.

It was a dark November morning. I shivered in the bitter cold as wet snow slapped me in the face. But with help from the Jews in my father's work battalion, I did make it through the hole and out of the cage unnoticed by guards. Perhaps life would be worthwhile and Edek, the long-nosed little Jewish cur could succeed as Edek, the long-nosed young man with a promising future. Perhaps.

In the succeeding months, the cage was crunched. Finally, in June of 1943, Nazis crushed it. They scorched the Ghetto and liquidated Jews in the debris of the charred buildings or transported them to available sandpits for destruction.

My parents somehow escaped. My mother found refuge with the elderly lady who lived with her seven cats in the garret of our apartment house. My father was caught and sent to Oboz Janowski, the local concentration camp. The cage for the Jewish community in Lwow was no more.

Chapter XII.   Silent Spring of 1943

"Do you notice how quiet it is now around our building, Donia? Isn't it eerie?" remarked Natalia.

They were both in the courtyard. Donia was breaking up a tiny parcel of hard dirt for onion seedlings. Natalia had come down to beat the dust out of a carpet that she carried under her arm. Once finished, she left it hanging on the horizontal whipping pole and turned to Donia.

"There was always so much happening, but not now. Do you sense it too?"

"Yes, you are so right, Pani Natalia. Nobody plays down here anymore. Your Lesia has nobody to play with. Kazik and his family moved away…Pani Yanka keeps Yacek in the apartment, mostly. And Edek…"

"Yes, Edek. It is horrible what they are doing to the Jews. I wonder what happened to the Edelmans. I fear the worse—I hear that they are liquidating the Ghetto. You liked them, the Edelmans, didn't you, Donia?"

"Yes, Pani Natalia."

"Just call me Natalia. I like to feel that I have a friend in you. I am not that terribly much older than you, you know."

Somehow the suggestion of intimacy with Natalia came naturally. Donia and her mother spoke with her infrequently—whenever they ran into her while doing their chores, like now, but always on polite terms. Natalia spoke Polish perfectly and used it, in spite of the presently pervading Ukrainian chauvinism which was promoting a "Ukrainians must speak Ukrainian only" ideal. The Laskawas certainly would have been more friendly with Natalia had it not been for her husband. Pan Fedan was an ardent Ukrainian nationalist and an unpleasant boor to boot. How she could live with him was always beyond their comprehension. A long time earlier, they had sensed that there was more to Natalia than her outward civility intimated. She smiled a lot but there was sadness in her countenance, a streak of unhappiness in her demeanor. Was she lonely?

"I often wished that you and your mom would visit me. After all, we live on the same floor. I am sure that my Lesia would like it also," she added, smiling.

"Yes, Naataaliaa." Donia enunciated her first name without the formal "Pani."

Natalia was silent for a while, jerkily shaking her head, apparently banishing a troubling thought from her mind and then, as if to reassure herself, she said loudly, "They won't murder all the Jews—they can't! They mustn't. My husband says that those Jews who work will be spared. They will be sent to the East."

"What about the children? What about boys—like Edek?" Donia blurted and stood up from her squatting position in the dirt to face Natalia.

Everything was quiet in the courtyard as the two females looked into one another's eyes. Stepping closer, Donia reached out her arms and hugged Natalia tightly, feeling their shared empathy for the Edelmans, an empathy that she could not share with her own mother.

"Natalia, please come to see us. Mother and I would be so glad."

From then on, addressing her as "Natalia" became easy for Donia. They now had something important in common. They were compassionate humans and they were young women—Natalia was certainly no more than thirty, but Donia admired Natalia for the years of experience she held over her.

+ + + + + + + + +

"*Haendaly, haendaly*. I buy what you don't need. I pay well. Give you good money." Pani Laskawa imitated the singsong of a Jewish junk merchant who used to make his rounds among apartment houses in the neighborhood.

"Do you remember, Natalia, before the war, when those Yiddish *haendelers* stood there downstairs in the yard and sang out their sales pitches while we stood on our balconies and argued with them about the prices of glass bottles, old books, and used clothes?"

"Yes, and we threw some abusive words at them but we didn't really mean any harm; we needed the Jewish *haendelers*. The few coppers always came in handy," responded Natalia.

Donia, her mother and Natalia sat in the Laskawas' kitchen and shared a half-liter of the sweet wine that Natalia had brought with her.

"What about the Jewish doctors? Remember Doctor Wilek Engelkreist, Donia? On the next block? And how he extracted your warts? It's a blessing that you don't have skin problems now. Where would you go now?" asked Natalia.

"Thankfully, for teeth we have Pani Doctor Ala!" said Pani Laskawa emphatically. Donia and Natalia smiled, nodding their heads in agreement.

Natalia reached for the wine bottle and poured a healthy portion into each of their goblets.

"She is not the same ever since Tusiek hasn't been here. She hardly ever comes out onto the balcony…keeps to herself. She doesn't welcome any patients—new or old ones," said Donia.

"She must be missing Tusiek's help," said Natalia. "That's why she doesn't do dentures anymore. She needed him."

"Professionally and otherwise," interrupted Pani Laskawa. She raised her eyebrows knowingly. Then more seriously she added, "You know that my Roman does her errands, but she seldom invites him in, and yet she was so fond of him."

"She was so friendly, but not anymore. Now she discourages anyone who approaches her. I wonder why?" Natalia said, puzzled.

"I have not seen her 'horsey' set of friends. If they were real friends they would have visited her. I don't think they are Jewish so they shouldn't have any trouble walking on the street," Pani Laskawa added.

"She seldom comes out on the balcony," repeated Donia.

"No one can see her even through the window. She has curtains on all of them," added her mother.

The three of them continued to discuss Pani Doctor Ala, but it was more a concerned curiosity than idle gossip. They also talked about genteel Tusiek who had left without even saying goodbye. Did he have enough strength to survive the Ghetto, he who was so pampered by Pani Ala?

Pani Laskawa turned to her daughter.

"You know, Donia," she said, pointing at a photograph of Donia's father, Pan Laskawy, that sat atop the buffet, "We must begin packing. We must begin preparing to leave for Krakow. I told you some time ago to see if our neighbors had a heavy sewing needle and sturdy thread so we could repair the torn knapsack. Natalia is going to see whether she has any. Did you check with the other neighbors, Donia?"

Donia didn't answer.

"Did you hear me?" she repeated plaintively.

Donia heard her mother but refused to think at that moment about leaving their apartment. Her mind dwelled on better times: noisy students in the middle school across the street; noisy streets with a lot of pedestrians, horse carts, and screeching trolleys. That was before the war. Now the traffic consisted mostly of army convoys rolling eastward. Not much traffic. Not much noise. No school, at least not for us Polish kids, she thought.

Natalia and Pani Laskawa began to reminisce aloud. The wine loosened their tongues and Natalia's open-hearted charm encouraged frankness.

"The gypsies were pretty noisy when they came into town," voiced Donia, adding to their recollections.

"Not the gypsy men, but their women who solicited to tell us our fortunes and their children who begged for coins. Remember the women chanting downstairs and jingling their tambourines? 'Tell fortune! Tell fortune from hand! Tell your life from cards!'" Natalia and Donia chuckled at her imitation of their accented Polish. The wine was mellowing the three of them and they felt good.

It dawned on Donia just how long it had been since they had last laughed. Days were lived mostly in silence. Jews and gypsies were gone from their lives. The new residents now occupying the Jewish apartments, as well as the old ones left in the neighborhood, did not talk about them. It was as if everyone felt guilty of their disappearance. She realized that no one really discussed anything with their neighbors anymore, except for superficial subjects like food shortages and the weather.

"I am so glad that you came to visit us," said Donia, as she grasped Natalia's hand when she stood to leave. Natalia nodded and gave Donia's hand a squeeze. Her eyes twinkled warmly.

"Here, I'll take the bottle. I may be able to refill it for next time." A tipsy Natalia reached for the empty bottle that sat on the table, but she knocked it over and it crashed to the floor. The three of them knelt down and began picking up the glass shards.

"It's a sign of good luck," said Natalia. "You see, Donia, we broke not only the wine bottle, but also the silence between us."

A few days later, the silence in the building was broken again—suddenly and startlingly broken. The painful screams and cries of Pani Doctor Ala and Pan Tusiek, and the abusive yells of Ukrainian militia and a Gestapo man who viciously beat them, reverberated through the walls and ceilings and echoed through the stairwell.

The mystery of Pan Tusiek's disappearance was solved. He had not departed for the Ghetto as everyone believed, but was being hidden by Pani Ala. Now they knew why Pani Ala had kept to herself and scaled down her dental practice: to discourage people from entering her apartment and discovering the hidden Tusiek.

Nearly everyone in the apartment house watched as large Ala was pulled semi-conscious by her hands down the steps of their balcony and toward the gate. Her legs dragged behind so that her flesh and the metal struts of her prosthesis scraped the cement steps.

The militiamen prodded Tusiek with iron rods and rifles. He bent over, straining to walk. Tusiek had a bleeding gash on his balding head. He stopped occasionally and tried to touch Ala, only to be once more punished with a rod. They both wore their habitual white medical coats, now stained with red blood. The Gestapo man and Ukrainian militiamen tossed them into the personnel carrier like two bags of potatoes. Tusiek desperately reached out his hands to Ala, to touch her one more time, to give her comfort one last time. It was the last that anyone ever saw of them. No neighbors openly condemned that brutal deed. They retreated back into their solitude. The silence in the building was deafening. Donia often heard the wretched cries of Pani Ala and Tusiek resound in her quiet moments alone.

From then on, the silence grew. They associated even less with their neighbors. Everyone was ashamed; everyone was suspicious. The Laskawas still had Natalia to talk to. Pani Yanka had Pan Burek and Pani Cwik. Otherwise, neighbors avoided each other.

"It wasn't Tadzik who denounced them," Tadzik's brother Bolek told Donia defiantly, his arms crossed tightly. Donia hoped he was right. It was hard to believe Bolek though, because a few days later, Tadzik enrolled into the Waffen SS and went to fight the Soviets, to kill Polish peasants, or to massacre the remaining Jews. Perhaps he did all of the above. In any case, Donia's former "dream boat" disappeared from her life.

The emptiness inside of Donia slowly began to fill with the multitude of tasks required for their move to Krakow, and the notion of moving itself. Her thoughts often turned to the

Edelmans, to Edek, to Tusiek. As the silent spring of 1942 ended and the summer reached its height, everyone was certain that all the Jews in the Ghetto, as well as most of the Jews in the local concentration camp, Oboz Janowski, had been liquidated.

As the hired horse and cart pulled away from the sidewalk with the Laskawas and their baggage headed for the train station, Donia turned her head back toward their former apartment house and burst into a torrent of tears. The neighboring statue of the benevolent Saint Anthony with the smiling baby Jesus in his arms did not ameliorate her bitterness nor her sadness.

Chapter XIII: Finger of God

⁓

Kurt + Natalia

"I am terribly sorry, Doctor Edelman," prefaces my neurologist, who then plunges into his diagnostic findings. These are not exactly news to me. But still, this confirmation of the steady decline in my mental ability depresses me.

"How long will I be able to function, Doctor?"

"We will have to determine how aggressive your tumor is. We will need some additional tests. The receptionist will schedule you on your way out."

Other questions form in my mind, but the quick assessment of my computerized medical record and the efficient manner in which the neurologist flicks from one display to another on his laptop are not conducive even to the barest discussion of my future.

"Doctor Edelman will need additional pain medicine. Would you be so kind as to prescribe it, Doctor?" interjects the young social worker who drove me here from The Blue Ridge Residence and who is now helping me to get up from the chair.

"Yes, yes, of course. Here it is."

The neurologist quickly takes his prescription pad, writes on it, tears off the page and hands it to the social worker.

"Be careful in administering it. It is fairly potent."

With those words, our interview is over. The neurologist exits briskly, leaving us with the physician's assistant who has sat silently during the interview and has now suddenly come to life.

"I will take you to the front desk and we will schedule you for an MRI. That is a nuclear magnetic resonance procedure that will give us a picture of your brain so that we can analyze what is going on."

Ignoring the physician's assistant, we slowly walk out, I with help from the social worker and my cane.

"We will schedule the additional test some other time," I tell my companion. "I want to get back to the home. I am remembering another physician from many years ago whom I would like to describe before my remembrance of him dissipates."

We amble out of the plush office into an elevator gleaming with metallic luster. My companion presses the button and the twin doors open noiselessly. Once downstairs, we amble—her steady hand under my arm to guide me—past the lobby and through the electronically activated main doors of the newly built medical center and into the parking lot.

"I will be alright now. It is fairly level here. I appreciate your concern but I will walk without your propping me up. My cane will do."

"That's fine, Doctor Edelman, but do lift your legs, with determination, counting. Like Celia instructed you."

"One, two. One, two. One, two, three." Then, "One, two, three, four...four, four."

"Four" gives way to "plus" and "five" naturally follows. My young assistant joins me in the recitation as we interlace our arms in a brisk march. I swing my cane with exuberance on "plus."

"Four plus five, four plus five."

"Why did you change the numbers, Doctor Edelman?"

"It has to do with a mathematical problem from my childhood. It was many years ago but I am still trying to solve it."

"I see."

I think of the words to the Polish national anthem but a mental curtain falls over them. The lesion on my brain prevents them from surfacing. So the rhythm of our march becomes the rhythm of the mindless, festive drinking song that the wretched brigade of my father's concentration camp was forced to sing on the way to and from work. Those abused, hungry, sick living skeletons at whom death stared at every turn of the cobbled road, had to sing it over and over.

"Ay wiec piymy chay, chay, checolade, czarno kawe, ay wiec piymy...rum." Let us drink rum, and...I hated that song but it pestered me my entire life and now it surges again with a vengeance. Drink, drink...

"It certainly is a happy song. Isn't it?" asks my companion, now fully into the catchy tune, repeating "ay, chay, chay" with me.

Before I have a chance to interpret the inane joy of the ditty and tell her of the cruel use of the song, we arrive at our van. Other memories eject the ditty out my mind. Hopefully, the ditty oozed into the nearby gutter, where it surely belongs, liberating me from it forever.

On the drive back, I try to recall a young Polish physician in a setting that was worlds and decades apart from the modern one that I am still a part of. There is no comparison possible between the Lwow of 1943, a Lwow brutalized by the German occupation, and the brave new American world of the twenty-first century. And yet, my disturbed brain keeps contrasting my visit to the neurologist and the visit that Dr. Joe paid us at the apartment where my father and I hid in 1943.

"I wonder and pray that, if our brave new, opulent world collapsed, the neurologist would emulate Doctor Joe," I murmur to myself.

"What about Doctor Joe? Is he one of your physicians? Is that his last name?" asks the young staffer from the nursing home.

"No, I don't know his name. I never knew it," I respond without any further explanation. The social worker gives up on me and concentrates on driving the minivan. I close my eyes and see my father lying feverish on the cot in a small room in Pani Helena's apartment, moaning in delirium.

My father's face showed two raw welts from the lash of a whip. His nose, a mass of dried blood, was unnaturally twisted. It had been broken.

Pani Helena knelt in front of the low cot with bowed head. Rosary beads were entwined among her fingers as she recited a litany to Saint Mary. Natalia Fedan sat on the floor next to her with her head resting on the cot. She was crying softly, perhaps also praying. In the adjacent room, Pani Helena's invalid husband Pan Bil held a worn prayer book unopened and he kept reciting The Lord's Prayer in a loud, steady voice. The words intermingled with my father's seeming gibberish.

"…must do it…they would whip me and use the guillotine…the SS would starve me in the hole…"

"Our Father which art in Heaven…"

"I had to save Helena…Edek would be discovered…you have to understand…"

"Matko Boska, Mother of God…"

"Which art in Heaven, save us…Thy kingdom come…"

"Forgive me…I had to break away…"

"Thy will be done, on earth…"

"Matko Boska, have mercy on us…"

"Forgive me…if you knew what these tortures are…if they brought me back to the camp…"

"Forgive us our trespasses, as we forgive those who trespass against us and…"

"…no, no…"

"Lead us not into temptation but de—"

"No, no! Don't!" My father screamed as if the whip of the SS man had lashed across his face again.

"We must keep him quiet, lest the neighbors hear."

Pani Helena turned to Natalia, who was caressing my father's arm as she held a cold, wet rag to his burning forehead.

"Kurt, dear Kurt, you are now among friends. The Germans will not torture you. We will save you and Edek."

Natalia moved her head closer to my father, who, in a moment of lucidity, placed his hand on it and stroked her hair. Tears appeared in my father's eyes, tears of thankfulness, I suppose. It was just a moment of consciousness because, soon afterwards, he began to hallucinate. My poor father was reliving his escape from a work detail four days earlier.

"Deliver us from evil."

Pani Helena's husband concluded The Lord's Prayer and the four of us, including me, said, "Amen."

Four days earlier, evil had nearly triumphed. We were delivered thanks to my father's sacrifice, and perhaps Pani

Helena's prayers. Pani Helena prayed a lot to be sure. Nearly eight decades of her life she prayed. But prayer was not the only component of her life. She was blessed by the combination of deep faith, hard work, and good deeds. Her blessings were good health, youthfulness, and absolute trust in God. Why did she risk her own life and that of her husband to hide and save a fourteen-year-old Jewish boy? Because she saw the finger of God pointing at me and because of a debt owed to my family from before the war. Her decision to protect me was thus made and sealed.

Through Pani Helena, I was touched by the finger of God as surely as God's finger is about to reach Adam in Michelangelo's painting on the ceiling of the Sistine Chapel. And so, after escaping from the terrors of the Ghetto, I made my way to Pani Helena's apartment. She put me into a tiny room where I lived in solitary confinement, unbeknownst to her family, neighbors, and friends. Nearly a year in solitude, until four days before—until the evening when my brutally beaten and diseased father stumbled through the door of the apartment and Pani Helena led him to my small room.

She brought water and an armload of towels. That, I remember. I also remember the bloody, filthy, smelly garments that Pani Helena took out of the room to be burned. The pathos and trauma of that day is a challenge to describe, but I must do it. I must think of Dr. Joe, for he also was touched by the finger of God.

Four days earlier, Pani Helena had left the apartment early in the morning with a small package containing some boiled potatoes and a few slices of bread smeared with precious lard. The food was for my father, who was an inmate at the Janowski concentration camp. He and about forty starving, abused wretches like himself were repairing a road in the area. They were all well guarded by Ukrainian police, details of renegade ex-Russian soldiers, and their sadistic SS supervisors. It would be a terrible penalty for anyone who approached them—certainly death to anyone who would give them food. Yet…

They are coming with the tray.

"It is dinnertime, Doctor Edelman. We have a country steak for you with fries and a surprise for dessert. You must be starved after that visit to the doctor this afternoon."

I don't want food but I pleasantly thank the serving woman who comes to help. Shall I tell the volunteer that I am sick in my stomach? Of course not. The visit to the neurologist and the memory of my tormented father, as unrelated as they seem, make me lose any appetite. I vividly remember Pani Helena. She was disheveled, bruised, and crying when she came back from her mission to deliver food to my father.

"Your father is dead. They beat him viciously. The SS man brutally murdered him. He sacrificed himself to save me, to save us. I prayed all the way here but…"

"What has happened, my dear? Kurt dead, you said? A tragedy—dear God! Will they come here? Are we in danger?" Greatly perturbed and worried, Pan Bil got up from the bed, entered my room and knelt in front of my cot.

"We all must pray. You too, Edek. Saint Mary will bring us solace and protect us."

I knelt next to my benefactor and, with bitter, salty tears soaking my prayer book, I joined him in a litany to Saint Mary.

Days later, I learned that Pani Helena had left the package of food under the designated rock from which my father would, at a later time, pick it up, unobserved. It happened that an SS man watched her as she hid the package. He grabbed her by the throat and brought the whip down on the side of her leg again and again and again as he screamed obscenities into her ear.

My father observed the scene from behind a tree. He quickly realized that the SS man would either murder her right away or send her to the Gestapo for interrogation. In either case, it would mean the curtains for her, me, and Pan Bil. My father had only one thought: to rescue us.

He raised his spade and menacingly advanced on the SS man, who released Pani Helena from his grip to concentrate on my father. He kicked and whipped my father repeatedly. Pani Helena saw the opportunity and ran away. The last thing she saw was my father on the ground and the SS man standing above him with a whip and a pistol.

The SS man did not kill my father on the spot. My father was sent under guard with the rest of the work detail back to the camp, intended for interrogation under torture and then a slow, painful death. On the way back to the camp, my father decided that it would be better to be shot. He bolted from the marching formation, hoping to be killed by the guards.

As my father ran into the maze of little streets in the old town, he heard bullets whistle by, but, to his amazement, he was not hit. He hid in the dark recesses of the ancient, tunnel-like gates of the old houses until darkness fell. Then he made his way surreptitiously to our apartment, where he collapsed. In addition to the beating, my father suffered from a high fever. From his delirium, it was clear to us that he also suffered from severe guilt: he knew that all the men from his work detail would be promptly massacred in the camp as a punishment for not having prevented his escape.

"Kurt is going to die. What are we going to do with the corpse?" It was a matter-of-fact tone with which Pan Bil spoke to Pani Helena and Natalia Fedan, who was visiting us.

"No, he will not die! He mustn't die. I will not let him die!" cried out an emotional Natalia, taking my father's hand into hers and kissing it.

I had suspected that there was a special relationship between my father and Natalia. Why else would she have come to visit Pani Helena ever since I had been hiding there, or bring gifts of food and try to cheer us up? *This* must be the Natalia that I overheard my father mention to Heniek. My eyes opened to the affection she displayed for my father.

"We must get a physician. We must not let him die. We…we must do everything we can," urged Natalia repeatedly, looking askance at Pani Helena. "To save him and to save you. We—"

"I don't see how we will be able to take the corpse out of the apartment without anyone noticing it," interrupted Pan Bill. "And who will do it? We need two men and a cart." Pan Bil had given up on my father's chance of surviving and thought only of saving us. Not so Natalia.

"I will go back home right now and talk to Pani Cwik. She will know a doctor who can be trusted. She is connected to the Polish underground. She doesn't know that I, a Ukrainian, know about her. She helped Pani Yanka and Yacek leave town ahead of the Gestapo, didn't she?"

"Yes, if anybody can help, it will be Pani Cwik. Go right away." Pani Helena turned to Natalia with outstretched hands and they embraced tightly. Natalia let go quickly, overcome by the urgent need for help.

We watched as Natalia shut the door behind her.

"And may God help us all," said Pani Helena.

Through the entire night, my father tossed on the cot, hallucinating and moaning with pain, frequently touching his crotch.

"In the last fourteen hours or more, Kurt hasn't urinated, yet he did drink. His temperature is very high," Pani Helena told her husband after a sleepless night beside my father's cot.

Natalia came that morning and a wisp of hope breezed in with her.

"I told Pani Cwik everything about Kurt…the seriousness of your situation, the dire consequences. She said that she would do what she could but that Kurt's bladder must be relieved immediately. Obstruction in urinating is one of the dangerous symptoms. She explained to me what to do and I will do it." Natalia blushed and ordered us out of the room. "Edek, get out of here. You must not watch."

I refused. "I will lay down on my blanket and look toward the wall." But I didn't. I looked and saw how tenderly Natalia took my father's penis out of his underwear and was pulling on it as if milking a cow's teats. Whether it helped or not, I don't know, but she repeated the procedure again in the evening.

Then Dr. Joe arrived with a bundle of worn out workman's overalls under his arm. Braving the night curfew, he came out of the dark, deserted street at midnight so as not to be noticed by anyone. He pulled out the stethoscope, thermometer, and other medical paraphernalia that were tucked inside the overalls and carefully examined my father.

"Forty degrees…very high temperature. How many days already?" He did not wait for a response. "This is typhoid fever—I'm sure of it. We must relieve his bladder."

He took a big syringe out of the bundle. He stuck the needle into my father's bladder twice and sucked out the urine.

"That will make him feel more comfortable. I hope that he has a strong constitution. Here are pills. Four times a day. I must go, but I will be back tomorrow night."

The following evening, Dr. Joe came out of the darkness again to treat my father. And the night after that. Natalia came briefly during the days so as not to arouse suspicion. She ministered to my father, affectionately and with apparent love. I even saw a smile on his battered face as Natalia kissed him on the forehead.

"What happened then?" asks the young social worker. I am startled by her presence. I hadn't realized that she was standing behind me, looking at the screen of my computer. I don't answer her.

"Natalia must have loved Kurt very much," presses the girl.

"Yes, they must have been lovers in the true sense of those words," I mumble in reply.

I think about my poor crippled mother, hidden a few blocks away. Was it my place to judge my father and Natalia? No, definitely not. Especially not now as I am nearing the end of my own journey. God selected Pani Helena. God selected Dr. Joe. God chose Natalia. They were His tools. God pointed His finger at them.

Perhaps my neurologist will be pointed at too, and it is my profound expectation that he will rise to the occasion—however perilous—whether on the battlefield or in the ruins of a city torched by nuclear weapons. I hope that my physician would respond to the needs of such victims and heed their cries for help just as Dr. Joe did.

Chapter XIV. Krakow, Poland

"I am happy that you made it home. Don't go out, Donia. I beg you not to go on the street again! The Germans are stark mad. They will do anything to defend themselves. They are ready to blow the bridges. Meinhard told me so this morning. He ran here especially to see you and warn us that the Soviets are near. You just missed him. Where have you been, child?"

"Too bad, Mama. I would have liked to have seen him. Did he say anything else? Will he come back?"

"Meinhard told me that the Soviets are on the opposite side of the Vistula River. They are in Plaszow. He and his troop are fortifying the river embankment. Don't go, Donia! Stay with me, my child. We will say the rosary together."

Donia had heard her mother's admonition many times before. Always "don't Donia," "don't, my child" and more don'ts. She was critical when her daughter looked amorously at Tadzik in Lwow. Here in Krakow, she objected when Donia went out with Andrzej and then with Smialy. Lately, she did not want Donia to see Meinhard, the *Wehrmacht* corporal. Wasn't my mom ever young? Donia pouted to herself. Doesn't she know how it feels to be approaching nineteen?

"Look at your father's picture, Donia! I love him and I am true to him. But you! You flirt and God knows what else with anyone in pants."

Just then a sequence of powerful explosions shook them, each one followed by a loud thud.

"Don't be scared, Mama. The Germans are detonating the charges under those anti-tank obelisks at the entry of streets. Remember? I explained to you after I asked Meinhard. Those tall hunks of concrete are designed to fall across the street when they are exploded at their base. That's what we are hearing, Mama."

"Thank God that the Soviets are not bombing us. But what are those distant explosions?"

"Maybe artillery shells. The fighting is getting closer."

"Will the Soviets be able to cross the river?"

"If they do, the Germans will fight them street by street and we may be kicked out of the house. I hope not, but we better put a few things in our backpacks, Mama."

"I wish our Roman was here. He is a man and we need him. Now they will fight on the streets—another Stalingrad. We miss your brother, don't we, Donia? Too bad he stayed behind in Lwow…Well, maybe it is luck because he must have escaped the German clutches four months ago when the Soviets liberated Lwow. At least I hope he is well…"

Pani Laskawa kept on rattling as she nervously filled and emptied their backpacks, trying to decide what to take. Every once in a while she looked up at the door, expecting soldiers to burst in.

"We didn't hear anything from Roman or your father. I pray to Saint Mary every day that she will protect them. I don't see you doing much praying, Donia."

"No, Mama."

Powerful, rumbling thunder suddenly erupted from the direction of the river. It reverberated for several minutes, shaking the doors and windows.

"Sounds like Germans are blowing up our bridges, Mama. Let me check what you put into our backpacks."

But they were not driven out of their apartment. The Red Army outflanked the German defensive positions in Krakow. After a brisk battle along only the main streets, the German occupation ended—at least for the Laskawas.

Meinhard was gone from Donia's life. He was a nice boy and she hoped that he survived the war. Andrzej and Smialy were companionable sex partners but, as she later learned, nothing lasts. She saw them occasionally and they exchanged greetings. They meant little to her. Her heart desired romance and commitment. She remembered Ala and Tusiek well.

"Donia, where have you been? I was beginning to worry. Did you sell much?"

No point to answer where she'd been. Pani Laskawa knew well enough that Donia walked her heels off on the cobbles of the bazaar in Kazimierz.

"Sold two packs and five singles. There is that one man who buys three cigarettes from me every few days. He looks like he could afford a whole pack or more, but he is more interested in getting me to bed than in buying cigarettes. He comes to flirt."

"Be careful, Donia. There are Jews returning. They are claiming the houses they once owned. They have money; they get dollars from America."

"Don't worry, Mama. He's not Jewish, and even if he were…"

It wouldn't have mattered to Donia. She actually liked her customer's dapper suits and manly looks as well as his candidness. After a few preliminary compliments, he plainly told her that he wanted her and that he would rent her a room in Kazimierz near the bazaar. He wanted to pull Donia away from under her mother's domination and Donia didn't mind that. She thought she might be more amenable the next time he stopped by. Right now, it was hard to pry her mother away from the subject of Jews. So few had survived the Nazis; yet the Jews were the subject of conversation all over. Talking about Jews was an obsession in Krakow.

"You know, Donia, that I am not anti-Semitic. But people say that those Jews who survived are the worst elements. They are not like the Edelmans or Pan Tusiek. They are like rats who are impossible to exterminate."

"Jesus Christus, Mama! Stop that! Now there are only a few Jews in Kazimierz and they have repossessed one of the synagogues. After all, many of them lived in Kazimierz before the Germans sent them across the river to the Ghetto and doom."

Back to the bazaar. Everyday vending her cigarettes. They were not really her cigarettes to start with. She didn't roll them; they were Russian brands. Secondly, she didn't own them. Every morning, Donia received a consignment to peddle, provided that she paid for the previous day's sales. On this particular day, she sold everything and could have sold more. Also, her admirer showed up with flowers and an invitation to accompany him to a new cafe on Honey Street near the re-opened Jewish synagogue.

"To health."

"To health," Donia responded and they clinked their small tumblers filled with vodka.

The cafe was a small eatery that faced the plaza. It was crowded with bazaar vendors who had finished with their day's trading. During the occupation, the building had been a warehouse, but it had been renovated and the smell of fresh paint intermingled with the aroma of coffee and sweet pastries. They were sitting at a little table for two, right on the stones of the plaza. Donia felt awkward not knowing her customer's name, especially since he knew hers.

"I know you are Donia Laskawa and that your mother is a religious Catholic. That's good. I made inquiries."

"But what is your name? What shall I call you?"

"Call me 'Rydz.' Actually that is my pseudonym, the name of our Polish marshal. I must not tell you my real name. I work for certain people and I travel a lot."

At first, Rydz was amusing and gentlemanly and he certainly had money. They toasted again to each other and then to his mysterious work about which he told her only that he had others reporting to him. She bit into some delicious hors d'oeuvres and suddenly felt his hand under her skirt, caressing her thigh.

"Rydz, please. Not here. Later, please."

"All right, but you know how I feel about you."

"Yes, but later. I just want to talk right now. You can't tell me what you do, but I want to know about you—anything, everything."

Rydz did not respond. He turned his face toward a threesome sitting a few tables away talking vehemently to one another.

"They are Jews. Look how the two men talk with hand gestures. I recognize the woman. She lives in the house where I am renting a room for you."

Donia wasn't startled by this revelation because she had already settled on beginning a romance with Rydz. Besides, the alcohol and good food made her complacent, blind to the evil in the world.

"That Jewess must have plenty of dough to pay for two rooms and a kitchen. They get their pensions from the Jewish Committee on Long Street. Jews from all over Krakow convene at the Committee building. God knows what they scheme there."

"Rydz, how old you are? I will be nineteen in two months."

"Old enough to know what these Jews are up to—especially now that Passover is coming and they will be making matzos."

"That room for me—will the toilet be inside?"

"The Jews will need Christian blood, children's blood, to make matzos. My people and I will have to stop them."

"Whom will I share the kitchen with?"

"A little more for the road, Donia?"

"No, no. I've had enough."

They got up from the table, he paid and they walked toward her future residence: a single room with a separate entrance from the hallway to the street, and with privileges to a common toilet and a bathtub on the first floor balcony. She also noticed an electric hot plate for cooking, which settled the question of a shared kitchen.

Months passed quickly for Donia. President Roosevelt, that "stinking Jew who sold Poland to the Soviets" according to Rydz, died. World War II ended in Europe. So did Donia's relationship with Rydz. He was a harsh man, full of hate and she found it was difficult to love him. She thought that they had simply tired of love-making by the time it ended. Donia kept her room but paid for it herself.

Hitler was dead, but not anti-Semitism, especially on the bazaar where she worked. As quickly as the time was passing for her, she was becoming disgusted with those around her even faster. Donia grew morose, cynical, and introverted, but she always visited her mother.

"Mama, have you heard from Roman lately? He should be coming to us. I am so tired tonight. Let's not talk about Jews—or anything disturbing, for that matter."

"Nothing from Roman and no news about Papa. I still pray, hoping that he is well. I was told that some Jewish people—"

"No, Mama. I don't want hear about Jews. Please, Mama, don't! Don't!" But she was not going to be stopped and, as it turned out, her mother's prattle was of profound consequence for Donia.

"Jews are returning from Siberia. Stalin is letting them out of the Gulag camps. I want you to come with me to the Jewish Committee on Long Street. We may learn something about Papa."

The walls enclosing the courtyard of the building on Long Street were plastered with paper notices. Those who survived announced their whereabouts and others asked about the fates of their dear ones. There it was:

Kurt, Sidonia, and Edward Edelman from Lwow are in Krakow. Please inquire with the Committee.

+ + + + + + + + +

Donia met Edek the next day. It had been three years since she had last seen him. He was slim—very thin, actually—and taller than her. His long nose was still a prominent feature on his handsome head. Severe lines were now chiseled onto his boyish face. Donia read in them the suffering he endured during those terrible years of German occupation. He looked much more mature, especially with his hair combed back from his forehead. His blond hair was longer now, and it trailed down to the nape of his neck. His blue eyes burned affectionately into hers.

Walls, that had penned Donia in for so long, crumbled. Torrents of tears flowed from her eyes. They embraced and their lips brushed against each other. In spite of his young age, Edek was no longer a boy. She felt the body of a man. She needed the love of a genteel man. She wanted Edek.

Chapter XV. One More Victim

The Captain + Letta

The spring and early summer of 1945 found the recently liberated Krakow in the throes of strife, violence, and uncertainty. For me, it was a season of shocking revelations about the enormity and bestiality of what became known as the Holocaust. During those weeks, Donia and I renewed our acquaintance, which was slowly blossoming into a romance.

At that time, I met Yacek. We happened upon one another at the bazaar and so made a date to meet the following afternoon in the park. There he told me his story and then left abruptly. I remained sitting alone on a bench, engrossed in my thoughts. He said nothing about meeting again. We simply wished each other luck and he walked away toward the old town of Krakow with its narrow streets, numerous churches, and the jutting remains of the city walls and other historical monuments.

I can still see him in his shabby suit and loose tie. His white shirt was faded and stained, the collar wrinkled. Yet there was dignity about him, an undeniable charm in his manner. Gently waving away several inquisitive pigeons, Yacek told me that his father was murdered by the Gestapo. Of course, I already heard that Captain Stumme did not survive the war. But why would the Germans kill him?

"Did you say Germans murdered him?" I asked, startled.

"My father was a Jew. It was in Ukraine, someplace near Kiev. They found out that he was a Jew," he softly told me.

Yacek looked at the lone remaining pigeon still pecking near the bench while thoughts raced in my brain. I was speechless. So *Kapitein* Stumme had infiltrated the master race to save himself, his wife, and his son. I moved closer to Yacek in order to hear him.

"My mother suspected that he had Ukrainian women. Probably one in every place where his outfit was headquartered. He was circumcised, of course. One of those women denounced him."

Yacek lowered his head and paused, and then in a barely audible whisper, "But not Letta. Letta must have truly loved him."

"Who was Letta? Should I know Letta?" I interrupted. Yacek continued, neglecting my questions.

"My mother died just over two years ago, about a year after you and your parents were driven out of our apartment into the Ghetto. It was after Stalingrad—in 1943. You remember that she was pretty heavy?"

He paused and I nodded, eager for him to continue the story.

"Then she began to use a lot of sleeping pills. That—and the alcohol—did her in. Mother supposedly had a heart attack."

So he was a Jew. Captain Stumme was a Jew, I kept repeating to myself over and over. Small wonder that Yanka lived in perpetual fear. She must have loved him. She doted on Yacek. She must have loved her Jewish husband. It didn't take much of an imagination to see Yanka and Erich Stumme—or whatever his name was—before the war, in their twenties. They would have been an attractive, dashing couple; young lovers breaking the religious taboo of their time.

I remarked to myself that Yacek never said "Germans," always "Gestapo." If he hated Germans, he gave no outward indication. Yacek was still the pleasant, inoffensive boy I knew when he was about thirteen. He was plump, then. Now, he was haggard and thin.

"When your parents were married did your father convert to Catholicism?"

"Yes, but only on paper although there might have been a religious ceremony during their wedding. I think that he did it for the sake of Mother's relatives. Afterwards, as a Catholic, it was also easier for him to be promoted in the Polish civil service. I don't think he was sincere about his Christianity, though. He even had me circumcised. Yes, Edek. Of course you wouldn't know it, but I am branded just as you are."

Yet another explanation for Yacek's behavior when I knew him in Lwow: he never relieved himself in the presence of other boys and he seldom played with other boys. He lived in fear of being discovered. How much more so did Pani Yanka?

"I do know, however, that he desperately loved us," continued Yacek. "In spite of everything out there on the front in Russia, he sincerely adored my mother. And Letta—you wouldn't know about her. I think that my father met her at one of the officer's bordellos on the front, but I'm not sure. In any case, it doesn't matter.

"Letta sent us a warning message from Kiev. My father had been found out and the Gestapo arrested him. A truck driver from my father's outfit delivered the note to us. Mother cried and boozed as she read it. Later, the Gestapo actually came looking for us."

"Did she know about Letta?" I couldn't resist asking, but Yacek just kept on pouring out his thoughts.

"Letta knew everything—even about us in Lwow. She must have been interrogated by the Gestapo, but she didn't squeal. She loved him. Letta must have loved my father; she risked herself by contacting us. She wouldn't have denounced him to the Gestapo—it must have been another woman out there in the East."

He could have easily said "another whore" but it wouldn't have been like Yacek; he never used bad words. He was still the same amiable boy, but I could tell that he was hurting. He twisted his body on the bench, as if the bench were an instrument of torture. His eyes began to well with tears. No doting mother to blow his nose now or wipe away his eyes, I thought.

"My father cared for Letta. And without Letta, we would have been caught unawares."

Yacek broke down and sobbed as he described Pani Yanka's bereavement—and his own—at the news of his father's arrest and disappearance.

As he was telling me about how he and his mother feared that they would be picked up by the Gestapo, my thoughts turned to the gory locale in the East: Babi Yar. It must have been in Babi Yar, the ravines in Kiev, the capital of Ukraine. It was the mass grave of two or three hundred thousand humans, maybe even more. Stumme must have been one more victim among so many. This is where the German Death Commandos were learning how to liquidate the inferior races. Erich Stumme did well masquerading to protect his family—at least for a while.

"Burek and Pani Cwik saved us from the Gestapo. They helped us to leave Lwow with falsified documents. Mother died just before the Soviets came, but I was liberated by them here in Krakow."

"Here? In Krakow? What do you know!" I expounded loudly, waking up to the reality that he and I both lived in Krakow and of being together in the park. Yacek wiped his eyes on the sleeve of his shirt. He turned toward me but was gazing past me.

"I am sick. I am sick to my heart to still witness the hatred toward Jews. And this time by Poles. Right here in Krakow! The same few Jews who survived the Nazis still have to tremble for their lives. They beat them on the streets. They pull them off the trains and…and shoot them! These are my mother's people. *My* people. Poles, not Germans. *Poles!* But you know about—"

"I am terribly sorry, Doctor Edelman but we will have to interrupt your typing. We have to take you in for another CAT scan. The minivan is here to take you to the hospital."

"Fine, but they will only confirm what they already diagnosed and I will lose precious time. Yes, I will get dressed."

"We will help you."

"No, no need. Please wait outside."

Yes, Yacek, I will never see you again. You walked out of my life that day in 1945. But as the magnetic field begins to activate the hydrogen nuclei in my brain tissue, I will think about you, your loving mother, and your gutsy father. And yes, about the girl Letta who fell in love with a Jewish man.

And so I do, as soon as my head is targeted in the CAT scan cylinder.

I think of those days when being a German officer gave a man absolute power over the subjugated Slavic people. I conjure Captain Stumme in the conquered Ukraine as he pushed past the other officers and soldiers and made his way up to the bar. The bartender was a thin elderly man with pale, slanted eyes. He addressed Stumme as soon as his eyes caught a glimpse of the swastika on his sleeve and the insignia of a captain.

"How can I help you tonight, *Herr Kapitein?*" he said in a very timid voice.

"Give me a pitcher," Stumme growled. He was restless. He wanted to explode. He needed something to distract him from this damn war, to forget about this man—scorched and godforsaken town—anything not to have this nagging worry about Yacek and Yanka. And yes, about himself.

Out the corner of his eye, he noticed a young Ukrainian girl waiting on some servicemen. The waitress was short, with light brown hair. Her frame was so thin that she looked as though she could blow away on a windy day. She avoided the stares of the men in uniforms who yelled their orders at her. Her eyes stayed focused on the small, yellow notepad onto which she was hastily scribbling their drink orders. Stumme watched her hasten to the bar and fill the orders. She did her job quickly and obediently, he thought.

Stumme wondered how obedient and accommodating she would be after work. He started to feel a heat rise up from under his collar. He was getting hungry and he knew what he would do to satisfy that urge.

After the waitress delivered the drinks, she returned again to the bar and paused to light herself a cigarette. Stumme walked over in her direction. She stepped aside to let him pass. As she did so, he stopped abruptly and faced her.

"You, girl, what time does this place close?" he said to her with a commanding voice.

She looked up and stared into his face. He had strong, powerful features. His dark hair and mustache gave him a stern appearance. The swastika band around his arm intimidated her. She did not wonder what he wanted. She exhaled, blowing a plume of grey smoke out of her mouth.

"In an hour," she replied in almost a whisper. She had a rudimentary knowledge of German; her pronunciation was awful but understandable.

"Good, then maybe you can help me. I have some supplies I need to carry over to my quarters and I will pay you for your efforts."

His eyes traveled up and down her body. Her worn dress hung off her like a wet rag set out to dry. Sensing his desire, she clutched the top of her dress with her free hand. She looked to the floor and felt a cold shutter wash over her.

"I get off in fifteen minutes. I will meet you out front," she replied without expression.

Stumme guzzled his beer quickly. He went outside and leaned against the building's crumbling stucco wall. He watched as drunken noncoms made their way out the door and down the darkened streets. After a while he lit a cigar and started to whistle a rowdy tune from his bachelorhood. Smoke billowed from his mouth and faded into the evening air. Minutes ticked away as he restlessly tapped his boots against the pavement. The bar door opened and the young waitress finally appeared dressed in a shabby gray overcoat. She stared at the ground, averting his gaze.

"I was beginning to think you were not going to keep your word. Here, you take one box and I will carry the other," Stumme ordered her in Polish.

She showed no surprise to hear a kindred language. She had met a number of Wehrmacht servicemen who spoke other languages. Perhaps he really is Polish, she thought. She obeyed and picked up the larger of the two cardboard boxes that lay at his feet. The box was heavy. She wondered what types of supplies or valuables the boxes contained. Maybe this man would let her have some of the contents. Would she be paid for her time?

Once at the officer's quarters, Stumme led the girl into his small, cramped room. He went over to a nightstand and lit a candle.

"Come," he told her. "Sit down here and let me get a look at you in the light."

She obeyed and sat down on the edge of a cot that was covered with a few thin blankets. Her eyes wandered from Stumme to the boxes that now lay at his feet.

"You are wondering what I have in them, aren't you? What if I tell you that I will let you have some of what is in there for a small price? Tell me, what is your name?"

"Letta," she replied.

She was curious about what her prize would be.

"Well, Letta, I have been a very lonely man, and I need some company. What do you say, will you keep me company?"

She looked at him and nodded slowly. Her hunger and her poverty would comply, though not her spirit. But she had to keep on struggling—and not just for herself, either. Her sick grandmother lived with her in a damaged shack on the outskirts of town. She nodded again, resolved. Stumme walked over to Letta and pulled her to her feet.

"How old are you, Letta?" he asked, still puffing on the end of his cigar.

"Eighteen," she replied meekly, staring at the wall.

"Take off your dress," he ordered.

She slowly unbuttoned her dress and let it fall to the floor.

Stumme stared at Letta as she stood before him in a pair of worn cotton panties. From the flickering candle flame, the smooth whiteness of her inner thighs appeared to pulsate while her panties shimmered as if they were made of silk. Instinctively, she covered her bare breasts with crossed arms. Stumme felt the excitement rising in him.

"Now don't be shy, Letta. I am not going to hurt you. You are only going to keep me company."

He reached over and pulled down her panties. He ran his hand up and down her thighs.

"Doesn't that feel good? See? I can make you feel good."

He ran his hands over her breasts, and bent his head toward her. He took her nipple into his mouth and began to suck on it. She tried to step back and he grabbed her face.

"You will do everything I tell you to, Letta! Do you understand?" he shouted. Then he pointed to the metal cot.

"Lie down," he commanded.

She obeyed. Stumme unzipped his trousers and ripped off his jacket and shirt. Hurriedly yet skillfully, he put on a condom, then climbed on top of her. She closed her eyes and felt him penetrate her. He rocked back and forth several times and then let out an explosion of hot air in her face and collapsed next to her.

"Next time, I will make sure that they give me a large bed and next time you *will* participate. You will do what I say, when I say it. Maybe next time I will show you how to please me with your mouth, then I won't have to use that damn rubber again. Would you like that?" he snarled.

He paused for a moment, then smiled.

"Next time I will take off my boots," he said, his tone a bit less harsh.

"Yes," was all that Letta was able to say.

He stood up and stretched in front of her. She had not seen a naked man like him before. She looked at his crotch and studied it for a moment. His penis looked thinner, sleeker. Maybe that is why it was not entirely an unpleasant experience, she thought. He was a hairy man, almost like an ape, yet he was gentle despite his brusque words. She felt the warm moisture begin to ooze from between her legs and down her thighs. Was it all his or did she feel the erotic release herself as well?

"Get up and get dressed. I will give you a treat."

He went over to one of the boxes and opened it. He pulled out two packs of cigarettes, a jar of marmalade and a candy bar.

"Here, you can take this with you. Now that you know where I am staying, you can meet me here. I'd like to see you tomorrow but I have to inspect a bridge in Poltava. I'll expect you Friday night after you get off work."

He tossed her the prizes and opened the door. As she stepped out into the cold black night, she decided she would not look back. Already thinking ahead, she wondered what present he would give her next time.

The loud buzzer penetrates my brain.

"We are almost through. Another few minutes. Please be absolutely still. Just another few minutes."

Yes, another few minutes in this damnable machine and but another few weeks on this earth—no more than that. But Letta and Stumme are still with me. And for them, the time was also running out. For them, there would be the next time and the times after that. Letta became fond of Stumme and she began to enjoy their lovemaking. Even sucking his smooth, slim tool became enjoyable to her. In time, she fell in love with him.

One night, the news at the bar held that Stumme had been arrested: he was a Jew pretending to be a German. He was cursed loudly and thoroughly maligned, and those who knew him—as well as those who didn't—were remembering what a piece of shit Stumme was. Letta left that evening before the bar closed and never returned.

A final buzzer jars me out of the past.

"Doctor Edelman, we are through. All went well. We should have good images. Here, let me help you to get down."

Good. My medical experts have "good" images of my diseased brain. I want the "good" images of Letta and Captain Stumme that pervaded my sickly brain to return, but they cease to exist.

In the succeeding days and nights, I think about the park bench in Krakow. I try to divine what became of Yacek. Is he still alive? Eventually, he surely must have reconciled with the tragic fate of his parents and with his own destiny: Son of a Jewish man and a Polish woman who loved him and helped him to survive. But what about Letta? As hard as I try to think of her, the Ukrainian waitress in a worn dress that hung like a rag does not materialize for me again.

Chapter XVI. One Less Angel

"Doctor Edelman! Doctor Edelman, please wake up. You are perspiring terribly. You are groaning and twisting as if you were pursued by monsters. You must be having a terrifying nightmare. Please, wake up!"

"Put a cold compress on his head, someone! You can see how the poor man is suffering!"

My deteriorating brain cells indeed evoke terror in me. I am being chased by several civilian hooligans, one with a fire ax, one with a table leg and the others with metal rods. They yell to bystanders: "Stop that Jew! We don't want Jews in Krakow! Get that Jew!"

They are a pack of hellish hounds tearing at me, gnarling and snarling with their fangs.

The crowd gathers along the street and threatens me with their gestures and screams.

"We will kill you like you murdered the Polish Christian children in your synagogue."

"Your blood, Jew, for the blood of our children!"

"You are not going to escape. We got you. You will pay for it. You Jewish Satan, we will finish what the Germans started!"

Some vendors are leaving their bazaar stands to join the hecklers along the street. A stout woman is spewing venom.

"They murdered three children, including a boy scout! Chase that Jew-boy to my meat stand and I will butcher him myself!"

Another woman yells at the top of her lungs, "You Jews killed more! There are seven Polish youngsters missing! That boy scout, Rysiu, is one of them."

Yet another: "A policeman who entered their synagogue saw thirteen corpses of children around their altar with their rabbi collecting blood into a chalice."

Yet another shrill voice, perhaps that of a young teenager, adds to the hateful chorus: "They grabbed me, beat me! The Jews were dragging me through the side door into their synagogue but I tore myself away and ran."

I am running as fast as I can, terrified by the avalanche of fantastic, vitriolic accusations. Powerful fear propels my legs and an unintelligible yell forces itself out my lungs.

"Doctor Edelman, you are screaming. You must wake up! We have to give you an injection. A sedative—you need a sedative."

"Celia, I can't hold his hand! He keeps jerking it. Maybe he will let you hold it and I'll be able to insert the needle."

"Let's try."

One of the pursuers is catching me by the hand but I manage to shake him off. With a frantic burst of speed, I leave him behind.

"There. I barely managed to give him the shot."

Just as I am outdistancing my pursuers, uniformed men appear from a side street two blocks ahead, cutting me off. One wears the uniform of a Krakow municipal policeman and holds a night stick in his hand while the other is a Polish soldier swinging a hunk of rope.

The house on the right. Just few houses up the street. The house I know well—Donia's house. Questions rush through my brain: Will I make it? Will they follow me inside? Is Donia home? What will they do?

I fear that I will endanger her, but her house is my only hope. I must—I have no choice. If I don't, they will beat me. As I run into the house, Donia opens the door from her room into the hallway.

"I heard their ugly shouts…the ruckus. I—"

I run up to Donia but she points to the stairs.

"Edek, keep running! Up to the first floor balcony. Jump onto the adjacent courtyard. Hurry, there is no time! Run, Edek!"

"What about you?"

"I will be all right…will explain…they will listen. Run, they are coming! Run!"

I run and jump, hitting my head on the ground. I awaken to a sharp pain jabbing my temples. The pain begins to diminish. I look around, but nothing is familiar.

"Celia, I think the sedative is finally acting on Doctor Edelman. Too bad that man is so tormented."

The next day, I am fairly lucid but there is a ringing in my ears. Not steady, but a ringing that undulates like the blue hills outside the window. The pitch rises and then falls. Could it be the telephone for me? No, there are no public telephones in Krakow. I fear for Donia but cannot call her to find out what happened. The local rag prints nothing, so maybe it wasn't bad. I fear to go there; if those hounds caught me they would tear me apart.

The hills become a deeper shade of blue, the valleys brown. They darken as the light vanishes. Now the hills become steeper and the valleys deeper. The unsteady ringing becomes a wailing siren—the siren of an ambulance that transports my bashed, bleeding angel to the emergency room.

On that day, those brutal fanatics beat seven Jews and an angel to death.

"How dare you come here! We don't want you. You killed her," Roman pointed his finger at me when I stumbled into Donia's mother's apartment in Krakow.

"Get out! It's your fault that they murdered her. They called her a Jewish whore and worse. They beat her without mercy."

"I love her. I wouldn't—" I broke down, sobbing on the stairs, punching my head with clenched fists and then beating it against the baluster.

"I loved her. Kill me, Roman! I don't care! God, oh God, why didn't you protect your angel? God, where are you?"

"It is you and your god that caused her death. Your fucking Passover! And spilling the blood of Christian children! Get out! Get out before I bash your Jewish nose off your filthy Jewish face!" Roman slashed at me with a coal shovel. I stepped backwards to avoid the blow and tumbled down the stairs.

+ + + + + + + + +

I watched from behind the tree as her coffin was lowered into the soggy Polish dirt. My grief scorched my insides. The few relatives present for the funeral services supported Donia's mother and Roman; they were all drenched by a sudden deluge. No one, nothing, supported me. My parents couldn't comfort me; they knew nothing about Donia's death. They had many other problems and I didn't want Donia's death to add to their burden. Nothing alleviated the pain except for my oath to build an altar for Donia in my heart. And so I did. Donia never left my heart. Perhaps soon our spirits will permeate our world together—from the soggy Polish soil to the blue hills of America and beyond.

"Look, Celia. Doctor Edelman is crying. Do you think that he knows he's close to dying?"

"No, I bet he is dreaming of those years long ago, Ginny. Maybe of someone he loved in his youth. I think that's what it is. I saw some of the printouts of the story he's writing. Her name is like Donna but softer; Doctor Edelman explained it to me."

I was not able to throw the earth on Donia's coffin, but anger is often stronger than despair. I lifted myself above my personal tragedy and, with a few hundred other Jewish men and women, I donned a black armband and marched through the streets of Krakow in a funeral procession, burying murdered Jews. We walked in utter silence behind the coffins of seven victims—victims not of German Death Commandos, but of a vicious Polish mob.

"Edek! Hey, Edek! I was hoping to find you here in this procession." It was Roman. What did he want from me now? I feared him. Both of us were very angry and despondent.

"I know that Donia loved you. She cared for you a lot. How can I make up for what I said and did to you? I was hurt…and so very angry. I could think only that if you and all the rest of the Jews were not here, this would not have happened to my family. I was wrong, horribly wrong."

I could not argue with his words. I said nothing. We fell into an embrace: an angel's lover and her brother.

With sadness and bitterness I told Roman that my parents had decided to leave Poland. There was no plan, really. We would go to the West—anywhere, just to get out of here.

"I will join them and we will start a new life, perhaps in America."

"Don't leave, Edek. We will be good friends. In a way, we are brothers now. "

"Get moving. Move on!" The rough admonitions came from the protective cordon of policemen, but we continued to straggle together behind the mourners. We walked in silence for a while, then Roman took my arm and hooked it inside his own.

Roman swallowed hard and began again. "I beg you to understand, Edek. For a long time, we Poles have used Jews as an excuse for our misfortunes. But never Donia. Neither will I, ever again."

"I must go. I must heal. I can't do that here."

"Don't leave, Edek. You will see that Poland will change."

"Please understand, Roman, that every building and every street in this town will be a reminder of this pogrom."

"If you must go, then take this." Roman reached into an inner pocket of his oversized raincoat and pulled out a package wrapped in an embroidered linen. I recognized it at once to be Donia's special scarf. He handed the bundle to me saying, "I thought that I might see you today. That's why I brought it."

Roman stood before me as I reverently removed the scarf. Inside was a sealed brown envelope. I ripped open the flap and pulled out several sheets of paper written in Donia's handwriting. The top page read: "Diary by Donia Laskawa."

The beginning words on the next page were: "I love you, Edek, and always will."

I stared back at Roman, unable to speak.

"I'm sure that Donia meant for you to have it. Take it, Edek, and forgive me—forgive all the well-intentioned Poles—for her sake."

"Keep on moving, you two. You are either going to the cemetery or not. Can't just stand here," our irate protectors admonished us again.

Holding Donia's scarf in one hand and the precious envelope in the other, I intoned the mourner's Kaddish: "Yit-gadal ve-yit-kadash shmei raba...b'alma..."

Hollowed and enhanced may He be throughout the world of His own creation. May He accept...my angel among His own.

Chapter XVII. Last of the Nine

Edek + Donia

"You will be fine, Doctor. Edelman. That will relieve your headache," Celia tells me soothingly as she withdraws the syringe from my arm. "I will come back this evening to see how you are getting along."

I am left with my migraine, my memories, and my laptop. I can barely focus.

At times, my brain perceives incredible scenes of the past. I think that my mind is perverting reality but I cannot be certain. It must be the damned brain tumor, always growing. The malignancy is playing tricks on me because the past is now the present. These last few weeks, my abused brain cells have re-enacted events—events so vivid that I experience them both emotionally and physically.

After the injection of morphine, I am not only an invalid storyteller from a distant time and place propped up in bed, but I am also young Edek, a seventeen-year-old Edek after the liberation in Krakow, Poland in 1945. I see Edek. I see him embracing a naked Donia. I am Edek and I am making love to Donia. But strangely, I am also Donia. I pervade her head. I know her thoughts and how she feels. Well, that's the way it is—or perhaps was. Does it matter? No, not anymore.

Four years before the beastly pogrom that occurred in Krakow in 1945, a thirteen-year-old Edek had already felt Donia's breasts against his chest as they held one another in the hallway of their apartment house and cried together after witnessing Mundek's murder. They were terrorized children then, and yet, in revulsion and sadness, they both sensed the unique thrill of their proximity to one another.

A week preceding Donia's death, what started years earlier in Lwow as an immature attraction became a fiery passion. Never before had young Edek felt such pleasure. Never before had he felt such desire. Donia had opened up a new world for him. One where war, hatred, poverty, and anything else he could think of, did not matter. Relishing the memory was not enough. He needed to have her. Today. Now. To taste her mouth, to touch her skin, to feel her heartbeat was all he could think of. Did he deserve to take part in such ecstasy? Yes. They both deserved it, but it had to be in stealth—and soon, before this hot desire consumed him.

That evening, luck befell Edek when he was invited to dine with a Jewish couple who rented two rooms and a kitchen in the same building where Donia lived. He decided he would invent an excuse to leave his hosts that evening. He walked out into the dimly lit hall and down the stairs. He knew it was the designated bath night for people in Donia's apartment and she would be the last one to bathe. He would stop her in the hallway before she went back to her room.

Donia exited the small bathroom wrapped in a worn, patched robe. She saw Edek and felt her heart skip a beat. Her thoughts raced back to that afternoon in the hallway. She looked into his eyes. She could feel his desire, and she wanted him just as badly. She needed to feel his warm skin against hers, his strong hands on her thighs, and his breath on her face. Without saying a word, she followed him out the back door rather than return to her room where one of her aunt's was staying with her temporarily.

He led her outside to the back garden. They passed the row of shrubs that lined the walkway. Edek stopped at the root cellar. Gingerly, without making a sound, he lifted the wooden door and held it open for Donia. She softly descended the wooden steps and stood in her slippers on the sandy floor. Within seconds, they were standing face to face. Edek reached out and stroked her cheek.

She was beautiful. Silver moonlight shined through the door from above. A holy whiteness enveloped her body. He slid his hand down her neck and she threw back her head. His fingers caressed her slender neck. He pulled her close to him with his other hand and groped for the sash on her *schlafrock*, untying it in a single motion. He opened the thin robe and gazed upon her naked body. She let her shoulders drop, allowing her robe to fall to the ground.

She wanted him to please her. She could feel the moisture begin to gather between her legs. Edek took his hands and ran them over her breasts and down her stomach. He got down on his knees and began kissing her stomach. She started to groan softly and put her hands on his shoulders. He glanced up at her and he could see that her eyes were closed. He ran his tongue lower down her stomach. Gently he began to kiss the soft lips between her legs. She groaned louder. He ran his tongue up and down and could taste her excitement. Faster and more intensely he kissed her. He could feel her weight shift onto him as she leaned forward and grabbed onto his shoulders for support. Her excitement was too much and she let out a small shriek. He could feel her body convulse. He threw down his trousers and entered her. Her backside pressed against a wooden partition and he could see her head move up and down with each thrust. He felt like an animal. He wanted nothing more then to force himself deep inside her. Beads of sweat ran down his back and legs. After a final thrust, he went limp. Still panting, he clutched her back and pulled her to him, resting his head against her shoulder. Nothing else mattered at that moment. Edek and Donia were alone, past and future swept aside.

And so I am with you, Donia. Alone, once again.

"Doctor. Edelman! Doctor Edelman, please wake up! Are you alright?"

The voice is urgent. But my head is still on Donia's shoulder. Not yet, Donia. Don't leave me, Donia. I beg you, Donia! I need you. More than ever, I need you!

"You are dazed. Can you see me, Doctor Edelman?"

I am your Edziu, Donia. I loved you. I love you so much. You saved my life but gave yours; yet, you were only nineteen—and so beautiful.

"Doctor Edelman, were you in a trance again? How is your pain?"

I feel a touch and then the jerk of a hand. Donia dissipates. Not quite, she crystallizes. Then the crystalline facets, still retaining her likeness, begin to blacken and blur. I am alone again, but I will join you, Donia. Soon, wherever…

"Doctor Edelman, please open your eyes. I am here. I need to take your blood pressure and…"

How can I explain to Celia, my visiting benefactress, that I would rather be Edziu than Doctor Edelman? How can I tell the nurse that there is no use any more of taking my vital signs? I know that I am dying. I want to die. I want to be with Donia. I know that my chronic optical migraine will not subside this time. It will engulf me in darkness, final darkness. My brain tumor finally conquers, yet I will end with a sense of relief: I am finishing the story.

I, the last of the "four plus five," am dying. Dying, but with Donia's picture in my memory. Right now, I want to leave this world. A few more words and I will be ready, but I cannot see anymore.

"Celia, please type for me…one last time…just a few words. I can't see anything."

"Yes, Edziu. I will be honored."

Did she really say "Edziu"? Just like Donia did? Did I hear correctly? My head is exploding and my mind is not functioning well, but I must end. Is there an essence to our tale? Yes, of course, yes.

"Celia?"

"Yes, Edziu?"

"You know what the story is about."

"Yes, Edziu."

"Can you understand me, Celia?"

"Yes, whisper to me."

She moves her head closer to hear.

"It was the cruelest of times and it was the most sordid of times."

"Yes, Edziu, go on."

"And yet, for the nine of us there were also moments of love, before darkness."

"Edziu, I typed it for you. Give me your hand. I want to hold it. Rest, dear Edziu, sleep in peace."

Epilogue

"Celia, please call the reception," said a voice over the intercom.

"Yes, who is it?" responded the woman who picked up the phone in the nurse's station.

"A young man," replied the receptionist. "His name is Brian Peterson. He is Doctor Edelman's grandson. He wants to talk to people here who knew his grandfather. I immediately thought of you and Ginny."

"I will be glad to see him. Please show him where the terrace is. I will be there in a minute. Thank you."

The Blue Ridge Residence was essentially a one-story sprawling building with a large terrace overlooking a forested valley below. Beyond the valley was a ridge of mountains and in the distance, a bluish outline of still another ridge. It was a beautiful and inspiring setting for healthy young people. It was much less so for those who resided here and whose days were numbered, thought Peterson, as he waited on the terrace for Celia to join him.

He stood rigidly erect. He was tall and slim, with blond hair and blue eyes. Just like your grandfather when he was your age, thought Celia, recalling the photo that sat on Dr. Edelman's nightstand. The fading photo showed a smiling

Dr. Edelman and his young wife cutting their wedding cake.

Brian wore a dark blazer over a crisply ironed white oxford shirt and carried a leather briefcase at his side. Celia could smell its newness. His knuckle was tense from grasping the handle so tightly. She reached out her hand to greet him and he switched the briefcase to his left hand then shook her hand. He towered over Celia. She had to raise her head to meet his eyes.

"Your grandfather didn't know that he was terminally ill when he came to us. Later on he was diagnosed with—But you know that."

Brian nodded.

"We were terribly sorry to learn that. My whole family was and—"

"Please, let us sit down, Mr. Peterson. We will be more comfortable."

Celia selected a rocking chair for herself and sat down, beckoning to the young man to take the adjoining rocker. Brian hesitated momentarily and then with measured movements, pulled a small wooden bench with one hand and placed it opposite Celia's rocker. He looked at Celia as he slowly sat down, placing his briefcase on the deck.

"Don't mind me. It's my training to maintain eye contact. I am with the prosecutor's office in Richmond."

"I see. I am ready for your interrogation," Celia laughed. "What can I tell you about your grandfather?"

"Well, anything. Only recently did I realize how little I know about him."

"You must know that he was an unusual man. He was creative…a painter, a writer. Oftentimes, he sat here on the terrace, right here where we are sitting. That is, whenever his condition permitted. I think when he came to the terrace he gained inspiration, a will to persevere…to gain energy to write that book. Did you read it, Brian?"

Brian nodded, "Yes, of course, yes."

"You are at most half my age, so I feel it right to call you Brian. Please, call me Celia. I would like that. Your grandfather called me that. Your voice reminds me of him."

"You probably wonder why I am here. I had to come. I had to know more. We were not much in touch, as you probably know. My mother visited him a few times during those three years—was it really three years?—and I never came by. Only to the funeral, but that was in Harrisonburg."

"So, that was your mother. Yes, very efficient lady…with a professional bearing. She is a lawyer, isn't she."

"That's my mom, alright. She has always done everything herself. I'm not even sure whether she asked me to visit Grandpa with her. Maybe I was too busy—"

The tinkling of bells disturbed him in mid-sentence. He reached inside one of the pockets of his well-pressed trousers and pulled out a cell phone.

"Sorry, this will take just a second," he said. He turned his body slightly as he opened the phone and put it to his ear.

"Yes, yes. I will be on my way soon…No, I won't be late…I'll call you back as soon as I get on the road…I have to go…Yes, okay. Bye."

"Sorry about that," he said, snapping the phone shut.

"I didn't spend much time with your mother," Celia resumed. "Ginny, my young assistant, did. She is due to come on duty soon and she could tell you more."

"I have an hour or so…Yeah, it will be good to meet her."

"You must be proud of your grandfather. He accomplished a lot in his life. He desperately tried to keep his mind active, especially in those remaining few months."

Brian did not say anything. He nodded and lowered his head. Minutes of silence ticked away. Celia glanced down at her hands for a while, then raised her head and stared at the mountain ridges. Brian kept his head down, his hands buried in his pockets. A few residents stepped out on the terrace briefly and then left.

Celia could see Brian's right hand fidget with the cell phone in his pocket. The time for silence had passed. She needed to speak, to fill the quiet with something.

"Now I remember. Your mother came to visit right after your grandmother died. Your grandfather was devastated by her death. We had to watch him so that he wouldn't harm himself," Celia paused, thinking of those traumatic times and how sorry she was for the old man, how she began to admire him, and then to love him. She thought about how Brian felt, how he loved his grandfather and had come to her seeking information that might heal some of his own pains.

"He loved your grandmother even though they were officially separated. I understand that she left Doctor Edelman just a few years before he came to us. But they used to call each other very often and discuss just about everything, but mostly family and politics."

"Yes, yes, I know. At the end of her days, Grandma was even in a worse shape than Grandpa. My God! All those years and I visited her only once or twice! But she did call me and we talked...she also remembered my birthdays. Oh, that reminds me—"

Brian bent down and rummaged through his briefcase. He pulled out a flat white package and handed it to Celia.

"This is for you and the other—"

"Ginny. Her name is Ginny. Speaking of her, here she is."

142 ⌒

A young woman in tight-fitting gray jeans enlivened by a bright floral-patterned blouse stepped vigorously toward the rocking chair, almost bumping into the sitting Brian.

"Sorry, I didn't mean…They told me that you needed me, pronto. I didn't even stop to change my clothes."

"This is Doctor Edelman's grandson, Ginny. He brought us a present. I bet these are chocolates."

"Yes, I hope you like them."

"I remember your mother well, Mr.—"

"You can call me Brian."

"We helped your mother dispose of Doctor Edelman's possessions. She mainly kept documents and photographs…and coins from his collection."

"Were there any special letters? Anything for me?"

"No, nothing like that. But he often talked to me about you, Brian, especially when he started to write the book, you know. He was fairly lucid then, but also very lonely."

"He also talked to me about his happy childhood in the bosom of his family," interjected Celia. "At times you couldn't stop him. I could tell that he would have wished for—"

As if wilted, Brian bent forward so low that his elbows rested on his knees. He cradled his head between clasped hands. Silent moments passed, then Brian recoiled. He stood up, tall and straight, facing the nurses as if they were the jury. He, not as a prosecutor, but as a defendant. With a tremor in his voice he allowed his feelings to escape.

"I am sorry about Grandpa being here with little support from us. I, too, lived in the bosom of my family, and I know that family brings comfort. But there were only three of them: my mother, my father, and my brother."

Brian's gaunt masculine face clouded but he kept his voice steady.

"We seldom visited my grandparents. I have only vague recollections of seeing Grandpa brush oils onto the canvasses in his studio or watching my grandmother at her potter's wheel. But during those moments, I loved my grandparents. I was proud of them, of being in my family—"

An intrepid Ginny unceremoniously interrupted Brian. "But your grandparents had a farm. Didn't you and your parent's spend some time with them? Maybe in the summer?" she prodded.

"A few times. But our mother was always afraid that we might get hurt if we rode the tractor with Grandpa or watched him cut trees. Our parents loved us and were always protective—overly protective. Even later, when we were older…Ultimately, there was my law school and work. But I could have…I should have visited them."

Brian grabbed the briefcase and set it on his lap. He was grasping the handle so tightly with both hands that his knuckles were turning white. Celia reached toward Brian and gave him a gentle pat on the shoulder.

"It is good of you to visit us. Are you traveling through the area on business?" She tried to move the conversation to less personal topics but Brian continued, as if in a trance.

"When we were children, we had summer camps, music lessons, school stuff—not much time to visit the farm. And even when my grandparents visited us we had our activities—even on weekends. But at those times we did, at least, have one dinner at home…all of us. My mother would cook…she was very hard working…well, breakfasts were eaten hurriedly…"

Celia tried to glance at her watch discretely but Brian noticed.

"I guess it's time for me to get going," he said in a businesslike voice. But instead of standing up and walking toward the door, he remained seated and fiddled with the briefcase handle.

"There is one thing—"

"Yes, can we help? Whatever you need." Ginny spoke encouragingly, looking flirtatiously at the handsome young man. Embarrassed, Brian turned his face toward Celia, ignoring Ginny.

"I wonder whether my grandpa discussed the book with you. Especially the end—the love scenes." Brian blushed, but his eyes remained fixed on Celia.

"Certainly not with me," Ginny replied quickly. "If Doctor Edelman consulted with anyone it must have been with you, Celia, considering how he liked you."

Brian noticed Ginny's quick wink to Celia.

Celia did not respond. Her face saddened and her eyes moistened.

"You mean the graphic sex between the Captain and that girl?" Ginny asked him unabashedly.

"He might have been hallucinating already at that time. During the last two or three months he was less and less lucid," interjected Celia, a professional crispness overcoming her emotions. "These love encounters must have been relevant to him. It's hard to tell. His brain was certainly deteriorating rapidly. He plunged into fantasy occasionally."

This time, Brian got up from the bench.

"Well, I really shouldn't impose on you any longer. It's just that I was told by a number of people, including a writer-friend, that those sex scenes must have been written by a woman."

Ginny looked at Celia, opened her mouth, but said nothing.

"Well, I must go," said Brian. "I'm glad that I got to meet both of you. Thank you for caring for him."

Celia extended her hand. Brian held her hand between his own palms and gave a gentle squeeze. He turned his face toward Ginny and smiled.

"God bless you both."

About the Author

Mark Strauss and his parents survived the Holocaust. They departed from a war-torn Europe and spent New Year's Day in 1947 in the middle of a stormy Atlantic Ocean. Strauss was sixteen when he landed in New York Harbor. Although the ensuing years were difficult for the new immigrant family, Strauss learned English quickly and forged ahead in his new country.

Strauss earned a doctorate degree in physical chemistry from the University of Cincinnati. He prospered as a scientist and mathematician, working at Massachusetts Institute of Technology, Franklin Institute of Philadelphia, and as a faculty member at Georgetown University, where he taught in the School of Medicine and the College of Arts and Sciences. Among Strauss's achievements in his field are his participation in the development of a problem-oriented medical chart and the creation of health maintenance organizations.

During his professional career, Strauss also worked extensively for the federal government: in the Department of Transportation, where he headed the Mathematical Analysis Division; in the Food and Drug Administration, where he supervised operations research; working on health issues for the Office of Economic Opportunity; and analyzing air warfare for the Naval Research Laboratory.

Strauss retired to the Shenandoah Valley in Virginia in the early 1970s and began a second career as an artist. His oil paintings and prints reside in many collections throughout America and Europe. In 2006, Strauss co-authored the mystery novel *Crumbs*, published under the pseudonyms Marek Mann and Maria Martell. *Four Plus Five* is his second novel.

Besides painting and writing, Strauss manages the Edinburg Gallery in Edinburg, Virginia with his wife, Joan. The couple has three children and four grandchildren.

For more information about Mark Strauss, please visit www.markstrauss.com.